UNDONE

FATE OF THE WOLF GUARD - BOOK 3

AIDY AWARD

For every woman who has to learn that she is strong enough
from someone else.
Oh, that's pretty much all of us.
So - learn it from me... You. Are. Strong. Enough.
Save yourself.

Is done an emotion?
   Because I feel that in my soul

— GEN X

TARYN

*I*n the beginning, I didn't know who or what I was. I was nothing.

Then I found love and remembered flashes of my life. At first I thought I was an ordinary human, nothing special. How wrong I was.

I thought I was a witch, because magic flowed through me, poured out of me, changed everything. However, like the men that I've claimed, the ones my soul yearns for, who I've fallen in love with, there is a beast inside of me. But it wasn't the wolf I hoped for.

No. What I am is far worse.

I look at the death and destruction around me. The chaos I am responsible for.

I am a monster.

And I've been imprisoned for the crimes that I disguised as courage and love. Maybe this is why I was thrown into the Nothing. Perhaps the people or the pack I belong to back in the real world were only trying to protect themselves from me. If only I'd kept my memories of this life, perhaps I could have controlled the beast, suppressed it somehow and saved those I love.

I'M HUDDLED in the corner of this cold stone and dirt room. It isn't much more than a cave, except for a few wooden support poles, and the bars of four cages that run from ceiling to floor. I don't know how long I've been down here, but it isn't long enough. Not until I rot away like the dead body in the cell across from mine.

The horrible magic of this prison island usually absorbs anyone who is killed here and knowing that even the island is afraid of this dungeon pokes at my fear like beetles trying to eat my brain. I know exactly who killed that poor soul. He was murdered, that I know for sure. No one gets sick, starves, or dies here unless they're killed.

I've seen the beast whose imprisoned me rip the head off a new inmate like it was for funsies. But I'm not better and it's good that he's taken me away from everyone else. That way I can't hurt anyone.

My stomach growls and I hate it for even thinking that I would eat. I don't think it's possible for me to starve to death. The island has kept its other inmates alive for hundreds of years, if Maggie and Will are to be believed. No one gets sick so I think that only deadly injuries can end someone's life here.

Or to be accidentally tossed into Hell.

The tears prick at my eyes, but I refuse to let myself cry. I killed August and Vas, sent them straight to Hell. The actual Hell. I don't get to feel anything but self-hatred for that. I swallow down the tears, but they roil in my stomach. Oh God, I'm going to vomit.

I roll onto my hands and knees and my body takes over. Dry heaves are my punishment now. I gag and my stomach rebels over and over. All that comes up is my own saliva and the thin spittle of yellow bile. It's more than I deserve.

"Feel better?" The voice permeates the stone and dirt around me so deeply that I can't ignore it.

I didn't expect to hear anyone speak to me ever again and his presence wraps around me like a warm blanket. One that I have to refuse, I must brush off.

You can't ignore me, princess. You can try, but I will always be here in your mind. I feel everything you feel.

Even in my current mode of disaster, the magic in me responds to his very presence. Every word he says, out loud or in my mind, lights a fire that as much as I try to mentally tamp out, continues to burn. It's pure, unadulterated arousal, and it's the only thing I can feel outside of the self-hatred and sadness.

I don't want anything to do with it. But it's also the only thing that I have.

I may want to die, but I also know, the Dark Prince of Wolves isn't going to allow that. He is going to be my lifeline whether either of us like it or not.

The mindspeak feels too intimate, but my throat is raw

from the heaving. The words come out hoarse and jagged. "No. I don't feel better. I never will. Go away."

I don't want him to leave me, but I can't stand being near him either. He reminds me too much of everything I've lost, or rather what I've destroyed. It's good that he's locked me away where I can't hurt anyone else. I crawl into the corner, wrap the thin blanket around myself and face the wall.

"You need to fucking remember who you are and break the damned curse." There is a dark growl in his voice and I track the sound of him pacing back and forth as if prowling in front of my cage. "If I have to lock you away for a century to make that happen, I will."

Remember who I am. That's what I've been trying to do. I've gotten so many flashes already of past lives, and clues to the life I'm living now but don't remember. I don't even know who cursed me with this amnesia or why. "I tried that and look what I did."

"That's because August and Vas were fools." The anger in his tone matches the despair in my heart.

Fools for loving me. Yet I can't allow the prince to scorn them or my memories of them. I let some of the power inside of me rise, just enough to give me the energy to stand and spin around, ready to yell and scream and beg him to leave me alone and never speak of my lost loves.

When I turn, the prince is right there, three centimeters in front of me, and the wolf glows red in his eyes. He pushes me against the wall and grabs my wrists, shoving them over my head against the dirty stone. "But I am no fool, princess. I know what you need."

He crushes his mouth down on mine and I don't even try to pull away. Because he isn't wrong. I do need him. I don't want to, but without his touch I felt so empty and alone. The moment he put his lips to mine, the magic inside of me shifts, bubbling up like it did before and filling me with both joy and power.

I struggle to free my hands from his grasp holding me against the wall, not to get away but because I want to tear at his clothes, touch his body and make him mine, just as I did August and Vas. I want to claim him. The need has been growing inside of me, I just didn't understand what it was. I do now.

The connection between us hadn't always been clear, but I've known since the day he attacked me on the beach, that he belonged to me. The mark he left on my throat only confirmed fate has ordained us to be together. But if that's true, why does he hate me even as he kisses me?

Just as he can feel my emotions, his are scored across my heart.

The prince's growl rumbles up low from his chest and if I wasn't already mated to two other wolf shifters I'd probably be scared because that is not a happy sound he's making. I tear my mouth from his and pant. My lower belly clenches and my chest burns with the need to be with him.

He snarls at me and buries his face into the crook of my neck where my skin bares his mark. Zings of pleasure go zipping through me and I want to beg him to scrape his teeth across my throat. I'm lost in a haze of hate and need. I whimper, much to my own disdain, and my hips push against him, searching for contact.

Boy, oh boy do I make contact. He's not just sporting wood, he'd sporting a whole goddess forsaken baseball bat in his pants. Or at least, that's what it feels like. My body isn't the only one losing control. The prince rocks his hips against mine and I can't help it, I wrap one leg around the back of his and make room for him between my thighs.

"You want me to fuck you right here, right now, against this cold stone wall, don't you, princess?" His tone and words are smug, angry, and needy all at the same time.

"Yes. I need—"

He pushes away from me in such a fast maneuver, I bang my head against the wall before I can even finish my sentence.

"What you need is to discover your own power and not rely on ours to help you remember." He says the words like some kind of chastisement, but at the same time his hand drops to the bulge in his pants and he strokes himself through the fabric.

I don't know how to respond. I both want to tell him to fuck off and at the same time want to drop to my knees and claim the right to stroke his cock myself. What the hell is wrong with me? Is this what hate and grief and fate all rolled together feel like?

"I've waited this long to fuck you, I can wait until you

remember who you are and what you can truly do before I claim you."

I'm sure that's supposed to be some kind of threat, but I don't believe him. This draw between us is stronger than he thinks. I don't know how or why I know that, but I have a feeling he and I have been at odds in past lives and still can't resist each other.

"I hate you." The words just come spilling out. I'm not even sure I mean them, but the despair inside of me has to come out or it will eat me alive. If he won't let me love him, I have to hate him. Those are the only base emotions I have left in me.

"Good. It's about time you do." He marches out and leaves me alone in the dark again. I huddle against the wall and rub my hands over my arms. I can see my breath with every exhalation and while I know I won't die of the cold, I can be miserable in it.

"You don't hate him, you know." A creaky voice comes from across the room. "He just wants you to so you find that place inside that fights."

"Peter?" It doesn't sound like him, but there isn't anyone else down her with me. There's still so much I don't know about the supernatural world around me, so perhaps it's his ghost?

"You thought I was dead, didn't you? I wish I was, but this damn prison won't let me rest in fucking peace."

Okay, so not a ghost. I crawl closer to the bars, trying to peer across the dirt room to the cell he's in. "You smell dead."

He replies with a dark laugh. "I'm sure I do. The taint of Hell has that effect."

Hell? "You've been there? Can you take me there? I need to see..." I can't finish my sentence, can't admit out loud what I know to be true. There's some spark inside of me that needs to believe that my men are still alive and surviving in that dark place.

But even that is too selfish. Wouldn't it be worse if they're stuck in Hell? What if they're being tortured by demons or worse? I shake my head hard, trying to erase the intrusive thoughts like my mind is an Etcha-sketch.

They aren't alive. I know better. No one could survive the demons on their own turf.

"You're the one who can open the shadow portals. Why don't you open one now and get us both out of here?" Peter doesn't cough or sound quite so raspy this time.

I back away. I can't do that. I'll never use the strange powers I have like that again. Instead of answering him, I turn my back and forget that he's here. Maybe he isn't, because he doesn't say anything else and the room stays dark and silent. The fetid smell of death wafts over from Peter's cell again and I gag.

I definitely want to punish myself for my part in what happened to August and Vas, but if what Peter and the prince say is true, that's not why I'm here. I'll never forgive myself for what I've done and the pain in my heart will never go away.

I huddle against the wall and close my eyes, but all I see

over and over is the demon wyrms, that horrible demon owl, and my men being sucked into Hell.

I shiver and shake, but not from the cold. I'm just so angry. Isn't it better to avenge their loss? Yes, I played a part in that, but so did the ones who threw me and all the others into this prison in the first place. The ones who must pay are the Volkovs.

I may not remember who they are, but I vow right here in this stinking cell, that I will destroy them. Even if that means I have to go to Hell myself.

I may be hurting and broken at the moment, but that place inside where my fight lives, has been awakened. By vengeance.

I may never be able to forgive myself, but I will avenge August, Vasily, and all the people who've been wrongly imprisoned by the Volkovs, if it's the last thing I do.

GRIGORI

*D*amn her to hell and back.

The moment I'm out of the half-dug basement of the old church where I've got Taryn imprisoned, I shift, needing to let my wolf out before my anger takes over. Or my own goddess forsaken lust. I pace back and forth through the ruins and rubble over her head and can still sense her utter despair.

And her arousal.

It's not even her I'm angry with. I'm the damn fool who kissed her. The taste of her skin lingers on my tongue and if I'm not careful I'll drool all over myself. I cannot allow myself to slip under her sensual thrall again. Fucking her won't do either of us any good. It never has.

This time has to be different.

Because I can't take losing her again. I won't. Enough is enough. If I have to deny the both of us the most base instinct we have for each other, I will. Even if she hates me for it. I'm supposed to keep her safe when she's at her weakest. But I think I've kept her weak by saving her from her own powers time and time again.

She's like a little sparrow trying to peck her way out of her shell. By helping her, I'm hating her. Making it so she can never be strong enough to live on her own. Why can't the others understand that?

Perhaps Vas did and that's why he sacrificed both himself and his vendetta against me to save her. I don't deserve his forgiveness, but the princess does.

I catch the scent of Joachim before I see him. He won't find Taryn here. I've made sure no one can smell anything but scorched earth and death here. *Go away. I don't need any lectures or religion today.*

He trots right into my lair as if it is his own. It is a church after all, it should belong more to him than me. He's the one who shared her need to believe in something bigger than herself. All I ever believed in was her.

But look where the fuck that got us.

He sits his ass down and looks around as if this is some normal social call. But there's no such thing when it comes to me. No one but Joachim ever comes here. Not since I razed this church to the ground.

No one even said thanks for finding the Volkovs' secret portal. Now it's guarded and closed to their machinations. I'm fucked if Taryn starts opening portals like she did in the battle with Nergal.

It's been a long damn time since he's been interested in her. I fucking hate fighting gods.

Perhaps you're not the one seeking absolution today, old friend. The bitter scent of her despair permeates the island. Tell me where you've hidden her, and I will tend to her grief.

How fucking right he is. I'm still not letting him anywhere near her. She needs to learn to deal with her pain all on her own. She's no baby chick anymore and I refuse to rescue her from her own self. She will grow as powerful as I know her to be. She must.

August, Vas, and Joachim have forgotten who she is and what she can do. They've made her weak, and I won't allow it any longer.

Fuck off, father. You're not helping. She's safe where she is. This time she does this on her own.

Joachim scratches his ear and looks up at the night sky. He's feigning his disinterest. He wouldn't be here so soon if he wasn't anxious. Or perhaps he needs company in his misery. *She cannot ascend without all four of us. I've searched for them, just as I did you when she sent you into the shadows to Hell. They're not there. They're dead.* Do you still believe there is anything to do?

She's already mated with August and Vas. My throat thickens and for the first time since Taryn died in her last life, my limbs and heart are fucking tired. Even if they were gone, it doesn't change my plans. None of us know what happens if one of us dies in this immortal prison. Perhaps we will be reincarnated, perhaps we'd finally get the rest that none of us have had in five-thousand years.

Vas knew there was a chance they might not make it when he asked me to take Taryn to safety. He could make that sacrifice because he'd already marked and claimed her.

He gave her everything he had, in every life he lived with her. No wonder he thought I was trash.

Even Joachim hadn't predicted Vas and August's sacrifice. No one would willingly leave her side once they were in her good graces again. I may never be. No matter how much I or the others want me to be hers again.

I don't regret not coming to Joachim's well-planned mating ceremony when Taryn first arrived in our prison. He wanted us all to jump through his hoops. I don't take orders from anyone else. I give them. It's when they aren't followed that everything goes to shit.

Which is why I've stopped giving them.

You still think she can save us all?

For thousands of years Joachim has been my confidant. Every alpha needs an advisor, and he's been mine. This is only the second time ever that he's come to me needing guidance. I hear it in his voice if not his words. He is once again questioning his faith.

He didn't listen to me then. I argued till I was hoarse that he shouldn't take a vow to a god he didn't believe in simply so he had an excuse not to mate with her. He swore it was more than that and ignored me. Why would he take my council now?

She won't have to. I will save them.

Joachim doesn't move, except for the slightest wag of his tail. He likes to think he's good at hiding his emotions. I can practically hear the litany of unanswered questions from him, but he's smart enough to answer them all himself without even asking.

Yes, August and Vas are alive.

Yes, I've seen them through the Volkov's shadow portal.

No, I haven't told her she didn't kill them when she opened a portal of her own and they were sucked into the mouth of Hell.

Let her suffer, feel her grief, and come back stronger because of her heartache. I can handle her anger and hatred for not telling her, if it means she breaks the curse on her once and for all.

When? I will go with you.

A third predator joins us and he is one I can't ignore. *As will I.*

William, the lion King of Scots, prowls into my domain so rarely. He wasn't involved in our battle with Nergal, so I don't know how he knows of Vas and August's fate. He and his strange mate always seem to know more than they should.

I answer them both at the same time. *The next time the Volkov portal opens, and no you will not. Someone has to guard it from this side.*

There aren't many I trust to slay the monsters from Hell, but the King in his impressive lion form can and will get the job done. We can't keep the portal from opening if a god like Nergal wills it so, but we can make sure nothing gets through to terrorize the inmates of Fire Island.

Last time I was distracted from my duty here, two demon wyrms emerged and it took me far too long to hunt them down.

Taryn still had no idea denizens of the underworld had been hunting her in the forest. Perhaps I should have made her face them and forced her to reawaken her powers on her own. I won't make that mistake again.

Will prowls around the church ruins until he finds a place to sit and begins cleaning his paws as if the stench here makes him feel dirty. *I will accept those terms. My luscious bride didn't want me going to Hell anyway. But don't fuck up the rescue effort, lad. There are a few too many women in our lives who will make us wish we were in Hell if you don't bring those boys back.*

One alpha to another, Will knows better than most what's at stake here. He's been around so much longer than anyone else, I wouldn't be surprised if he knew who and what Taryn is. Even if he doesn't, his mate is special enough, that he understands what it means to be in love with a powerful woman that the rest of the world wants to destroy.

Fuck. I am not in love with Taryn. Not this time. I can't afford to be.

This reincarnated life of hers has to be different, and I'm the only one who seems to understand that. We've been doing the same thing for thousands of years, over and over. We find where she'd been hidden away, work to protect her, keep her safe, help her discover her true self and the power within, and then she is taken from us and we have to start from scratch in her next life.

No more. The Volkovs have made too many mistakes that I will take advantage of, and if I have to drag the rest of the Wolf Guard kicking and screaming into my plan, fine. I may have forsaken my position as their alpha, but that doesn't mean I don't still know their strengths and weaknesses or how to control them.

If a trip to Hell and back doesn't change their minds, my prison for them will.

What would you have me do with Taryn while you're off saving the world? Joachim's tone is a bit more snide than I'm used to hearing from him. He's always been the peacemaker and doesn't pick fights. He's more cunning, but no less of a warrior.

You'll stay away from her. She doesn't need to be coddled. He had his chance and once again denied himself and Taryn that comfort. Too late now.

I wait for his rebuttal, but none comes. Good. I don't want to argue with him. No doubt this isn't the end of it. Joachim has machinations of his own that I've never understood. He'll search for her, but I'm ready for him. He won't like the plans I have.

In the end, when Taryn ascends to her rightful place once again, they'll thank me. *Go away, you won't find her here. Tend to your sheep in wolves' clothing. They're the flock that needs a man of the cloth and the platitudes of a messenger of God.*

I full well know that he'll look for her. In fact, I'm counting on it. With the bait laid out for him and my trap ready to spring, I'm done with talk and still have this angry energy to burn off. I hadn't planned on going through the portal so soon, but what better way to work through the feelings I don't want to acknowledge than by destroying minions of hell?

Joachim doesn't budge and simply sits there staring at me. I can't give him what he wants, because he wants me to be something better than I am. That's what he's always wanted for all of us. But with each life, he gets more and more desperate.

Perhaps that's why he twisted the way he interacted with her. He no longer fulfilled his duty to her by being her mate. How is what I do now any different? I no longer serve her as the alpha of the Wolf Guard. I cannot be her lover as much as I want her.

Huh. For the first time since Joachim took his stupid vows and decided to forsake her bed, I understand his decision. Yet, he condemns mine even as he tries to find forgiveness for me.

Well, he was going to have plenty of time to ponder his mistakes, and mine, once he is imprisoned and can no longer manipulate Taryn's life... or mine.

I'm going to make sure there are no traces of Taryn's portals. Be gone when I return. I turn my back on him and trot off into the forest, toward the chapel in the woods, not wanting anymore talk. Will has never cared about manners, so it's not as if my abrupt end to the conversation will offend him. He may not know the details, but he inherently knows what I have to do will be both hard and the right thing.

I hear the two of them moving around my lair. Joachim didn't even wait for me to get very far away before he defied my orders not to search for Taryn. He won't find her this time. But he'll be back.

When I get back from this foray into Hell, I suspect he'll be waiting in a cell alongside Taryn. A strange pang spreads across my chest. I have no right to be hurt that Joachim is trying to rescue Taryn from me. In fact, I planned on him doing just that.

He, August, and Vas are the ones who suffered because of me. At any time I could have used my alpha voice to command them to my will. I may have abdicated my position, but in truth, they are still my pack, and I, their alpha. Taryn ensured long ago that the four of us would always be bound both to her and each other.

Not even my anger can break that bond.

About ten minutes after leaving Joachim and Will in my lair, I sense a new presence on the island. It doesn't have a scent, and I don't even know which direction to go to stalk this being. But I know that it isn't wolf, isn't human, isn't good.

Something evil has come to Fire Island, and it's my responsibility to destroy it.

Until Taryn ascends and then her light will destroy all the darkness and evil once again. Just like it did for our people five-thousand years ago.

TARYN

*I*f I'm going to avenge the death of my mates, the first thing I have to do is get the hell out of this stinking dungeon. Who has a dungeon, anyway. It's not like I'm a Disney princess locked away in a tower by an awful beast. Well, the Dark Prince of Wolves is pretty beastly.

I doubt true love's kiss can save him.

Doesn't mean I don't want to kiss him.

Ack. What is wrong with me. He's a complete douchepotato and I should want nothing to do with him. So why in the world does he make my girly bits go all tingly even thinking about him?

I don't want to admit that I already know.

He's mine. Just the same as August, Vasily, and Joachim are. I can't have Father Joachim either, and I've lost August and Vas to the depths of Hell.

Fine. It's fine. I'll be fricking fine.

I will figure out what to do about the tornadoes of emotion I'm having about all my wolves later. I can't think about that now. I'll think about it tomorrow. For today, or tonight, I can't tell what time of day it is in all this darkness, I will simply focus on finding a way out of this prison within a prison.

"Hey Peter, any chance you know of an escape route?"

He doesn't answer. What a creep. Ooh, or maybe he's really dead this time? He didn't sound great when I was talking to him earlier. That's just got to be another thing I can't think about right now. Get out. That's all I can do. I'll send help back for Peter if I can escape and get back to the *derevnya*.

There are real bars on two sides of my cell and the others are dirt and stone walls as if this place is simply a big hole dug into the ground. I shake the bars, but they don't budge. I drop to my knees and scrape at the dirt beneath me. If I can find the bottom, I could dig underneath. Like a dog, or a wolf.

This whole shifting thing is still so new to me and I sometimes forget. I take a moment to clear my mind and pull up the emotions that Vas taught me. I think of him and his unwavering love and devotion to me, I think of August and the way his arms and body felt wrapped around mine. There is the warmth and passion of their love for me and mine for them. Those are supposed to be the ones I use to shift back to my human form, but I know what's coming next.

The tear in my heart pains me just as if the stupid thing has been torn from my chest again. The wolftresses rises up just as she did when Vas taught me how to embrace this other form. Sparkling blue light, my magic, rushes over me and for a moment this underground prison is illuminated.

If I weren't in the middle of shifting, I'd throw up. There are bones, human bones scattered everywhere in three other cells. How many people have died down here?

I can't think about that now. I am not god-damn dying down here. I've got shit to do.

In wolf form my senses are overwhelmed with the stench of this place. It's more than death. If I had to guess, this is what brimstone smells like. I push away the thoughts that the Dark Prince of Wolves got his darkness from Hell. He protected and saved me from the demons, even if I didn't want him too. I watched him destroy them, ripping them apart until they turned to oily stains in the beautiful natural chapel.

If he was in league with them, I don't think he would have killed as many as he did. But what do I know?

I ignore the worries and set to digging. One by one my claws break off on the earth here that is frozen hard like cement. It's impenetrable permafrost. After fifteen minutes my paws are bloody and I've hardly made any progress. There's nothing more than a slight depression in the dirt. I shift back, avoiding looking around when my magic lights up the room again.

This digging out idea isn't going to work. Okay, maybe digging up?

I crawl up onto the makeshift wooden cot and scratch as high up as I can reach. My fingers are bloody in my human form too from my nails being torn off and I'll I do is leaves smears of dark red on the stone. If it's even possible, the dirt here is even harder than on the floor. This plan to quickly dig hole in the ground or the wall to escape isn't going to work. The dirt has been compacted and the bars are solid immovable objects. Without someone else coming to my rescue, I'm not getting out of here.

Unless I open another portal.

A shiver that has nothing to do with the cold ripples through me. I can't. I won't ever use that kind of magic again.

But if I can open a portal into hell, couldn't I use my magic to open some stupid jail cell bars? I wish there was someone around who could teach me more about where my magic comes from and how to use it. Where's a Hogwarts when you need one. Ooh, another thing I've just remembered. I used to like to read. A lot. That was my escape.

If I'm stuck on this stupid prison island for the rest of an eternal life, and I hope I'm not, I'm going to start writing books. Romances between women who aren't perfect, in their minds or bodies but who are kinda badass anyway, like me, and some super schmexy wolf shifters. Hmm. Maybe I'll start doing that if we all get out of this supernatural prison anyway.

At least that will give me something to think about other than stewing and being sad or mad, or smad, like before while I'm stuck here in the dark. Wait, no, I don't want to think that way. I will get out of here. Then I'll kick the Dark Prince of Wolves delicious butt, and go rescue my mates. Just putting that out into the universe.

After several deep breaths, I close my eyes and search inside of myself for the magic inside of me. This time, it's easier to find that then it is was to find the wolf. The blue light flickers in my mind and I imagine it working it's way down my arms and bursting from my fingertips.

When I peek one eye open, there is indeed, tiny sparkles of blue shimmering from my fingertips. It's not as strong as when I was in the fight against that owl demon thing and trying to open portal. This is more like I've stuck my fingers in a pot of blue glitter. But it's going to have to do, because that's all I've got in me at the moment.

I wiggle my fingers and waved my hand back and forth over the bars and imagined them splitting open wide enough for me to walk though. The bars creaked and groaned and I mentally pushed harder. Is there a wider space between the two metal rods in front of me, or am I imagining it?

"That's not going to work," Peter's voice croaks out from the other side of the room.

Poof. He's broken my concentration and into my self-doubt. The magic fades away and I drop down onto my knees. That push sucked out every last drop of energy I had and now I have a headache. When we were out in the moonlight before, I could feel the drain, but the night air seemed to refill me. Here in the cold, damp darkness, it's like I can't breathe.

"Don't be a dick, Peter." I need people around me who believe in me, not haters. He doesn't respond so maybe he's learned his lesson. Or he's dead. He really smells dead.

I'm not giving up yet, but I don't think I can keep trying to escape until I rest, and hopefully get some food and water. Will the Dark Prince even give me those basic necessities? I can't I even starve to death or die of dehydration on this horrible immortal prison island, but I can feel the effects of it on my body.

I both want the Dark Prince to come back and the thought of seeing him makes me shiver. I want to wrap myself up in him, and never want to see him again, all at the same time.

I bow my head and do my best to conserve my energy. I don't know how long I'll have to wait, but I can do nothing else. A hundred scenarios run through my mind of what will happen when the Dark Prince returns. If he ever does. I can try to seduce him, or beg, or cry, or fight.

I don't think any of them will work. What I need is help. Then as if I manifested what I wanted, I hear a scratching above my head and am immediately on my feet. "Hello? Is anyone there? Help me, help."

That was probably dumb. I'm sure it's just my captor again, but if it isn't, I'm not missing the opportunity to be rescued. I may be powerful and working my way into being the badass everyone else seems to think I am, but there's no shame in getting help, especially when it's dire freaking straights.

"Please, anyone. I'm down here." I pound against the wall, which doesn't do much, so I run over to the metal bars. Running my fingers back and forth across them also doesn't make much sound and I needed a racket. There's nothing in my cell to help. What I need is a tin cup to bang against the bars like they do in the old movies.

I search the cell quickly and there's nothing in here that will work. The Dark Prince must have cleared it out especially for me. But the cell next to mine has those bones. Oh God - sorry father - I have to get one, pick it up, and bang it against the metal, or I have no chance of being heard.

I swallow hard and turn to the set of bars separating my cell from the next. There's a skull, but thankfully it's all the way on the other side and I couldn't reach it even if I wanted to. The only one that is within reach is a handful of small bones that seem as if they're pointing right at me. This was someone's hand. Someone big, because the whole thing is twice the size of mine, even with my skin and muscle still intact.

But still, even the largest bone will barely be big enough to work like I want. I quickly grab two of the biggest of the bunch, trying not to think about who this might have been, and drag them back and forth across the metal bars like a macabre xylophone. "Can anybody hear me? I'm down here. Help me, please."

I paused for a moment to see if I could hear the

scratching or any other movement above again. Everything was deadly silent. Crapballs.

But then a sliver of light shot into the darkness from the stairway. "Taryn, quiet. I am here for you."

Oh my God - sorry Father - I'm saved. It's Father Joachim, in the flesh. When the Dark Prince ripped me from the battle with the evil owl demon and those horrible oily wyrms I didn't know if he'd survived. I'm so happy to see him, that I could pee my pants. Except I'm not wearing any.

I shout whisper to him, "Hurry, I don't know if there are keys or what. It's so dark down here and you do not want to see what it looks like in the light."

Father Joachim doesn't hurry. He squints his eyes and looks around as if there are a hundred booby traps. I'm pretty sure I have the only two boobs in this place. I wave him over and he creeps forward, sniffing the air. "Taryn, are you alright?"

"Yes, mostly. I'm more mentally hurt than physically." I look down at my hands, but the wounds from digging are all healed up. "That's Peter you're smelling."

"No, there is something worse down here than a rotting corpse."

"You gotta get me out of here so we can open another portal to hell, and..." I don't have the guts to ask him if he knows what Vas and August's fates are. When we get back to the derevnya, and I can safely curl up in his arms, then he can tell me the truths of what I've done.

He still isn't moving faster than an exhausted sloth. I've

never seen him so cautious before. His wolf is shining in his eyes and the sliver of light from the stairwell allows me to see that he's fingering the prayer beads at his waist. That one singular ray of light is heaven sent.

"Come on, Father. Before the Dark Prince comes back."

Once again, as if I conjured him, the Prince's shadow blots out the light. I know it's his because I can feel his presence from my skin to my soul. "Too late."

Father Joachim spins to face our nemesis, but the trap-door at the top of the stairs slams shut enveloping us all again in utter darkness. All I can see now is Father Joachim's glowing blue eyes. "Hide, Taryn, now."

His words barely make it out of his mouth before he drops his robes and shifts into his wolf. But before his paws even hit the dirt, he's thrown across the room. I scream because I don't know what else to do.

Crap. Duh. I shift into my wolf form too, and now with my wolf's vision I can once again make out shapes. But where I expect to see the Dark Prince and Father Joachim fighting, there is nothing. Like... Nothing. The next cell over where the father was thrown is filled with the black fog that I was held captive in before the island. The fog that stole all my memories.

I snarl and bring up the magic inside of me. I don't have much left, but what I do have explodes out of me in so many rays of light. It pushes the Nothing back, as if it's a sentient being retreating in pain. Good. Fuck off you disgusting bit of evil.

It finally dissipates enough that I can see Father

Joachim's wolf lying prone in the next cell over. I hurry over and snick my snout through the bars between us. *Can you hear me, Father?*

I don't even know if he and I can mindspeak like I can with the others. Father Joachim has never marked me, although we've done some stuff that only mates would do with each other, so I'm hoping.

He doesn't respond, not even a twitch. But I don't know if it's because he can't hear me or because he's hurt that bad. He's not dead. He can't be dead, I would know. I. Would. Know.

I shift back because there's nothing I can do as a wolf if he can't hear me and maybe I can reach my arm through and try to at least touch him so he knows I'm here. Even stretching as far as I can, I can only barely get a hand into the tips of his scruff.

But I can see feel the up and down movement of his breathing and that makes me feel loads better. Finally after a few moments he shifts and moves closer to me. He's still not awake, but he must have sensed my presence. I stroke the back of his neck until I come across something strange, stuck in his fur.

Carefully I untangle it, hoping it's not like a blood clot or something. I haven't felt any other bleeding, but maybe I missed something. When I finally get the thing out, I pull something that's hard like a stick, but covered in something soft. When I get it close enough to my face to see what it is, I'm holding a black feather.

Just like the evil owl.

Gulp. The Dark Prince of Wolves saved me from the battle with that demon. This must just be a leftover feather from when Father Joachim was fighting too.

The Dark Prince couldn't be in league with Hell. Not if he was one of my mates. Damn it. I was going to have to save him too, wasn't I?

GRIGORI

*F*ather forgive me for what I've done.

That's what I should be thinking. But I'm not. The feelings running through my blood as I lock the hidden trapdoor to my secret dungeon tight is not remorse. Hmm. This is more like a good old-fashioned gloat.

It took a good amount of work and planning to set a trap for one of the Wolf Guard. Only in the wake of Taryn's destruction would he have been vulnerable enough to get caught. But I used bait he could never resist.

Joachim can resist anything but temptation. And temptation's name is Taryn.

He'll spend his time comforting her guilt because it means he can avoid thinking about his own. The two of them together tucked away safe in my dungeon gives me the breathing room I need to attempt to rescue August and Vas.

I fucking hate Hell, and I don't want to go. But I will. For her.

I shake my head to clear away the thoughts of her in the dark, awaiting her fate. Will she remember the last time she was trapped in a damp dark basement? I would spare her those memories if I could. They haunt me every time I see her.

A hundred plus years imprisoned on this island isn't enough to forget the last time she died. In my arms, by my own hands.

Father Joachim thinks he has guilt. Over what I don't know. But he doesn't know what it means to kill your beloved. He could never do what I had to that day. I can never forgive myself or the Volkovs for letting the Bolsheviks run roughshod over the last Wolf Tzar to rule over Russia. Even if Nikolai Alexandrovich Romanov was the worst kind of idiot, and his wife a cheating whore, their children didn't deserve to die that way.

I should have fucking known Rasputin would get his revenge.

There was no way I was going to allow my sweet Anastasia to be... no. I couldn't even think about what they would have done to her if I hadn't taken her life first.

Enough. It's been too long since I allowed those memories to crawl into my brain like flesh-eating scarabs. I made the choices I did, and it didn't matter if no one ever forgave me. Including myself. That wasn't what mattered now.

I may not let him know that I agreed with him, but Joachim was right. Taryn couldn't ascend and take her rightful place unless all four of us were here to guard her. Without August and Vas, we were incomplete and she would never rise again.

I cover the trapdoor so no one else can find it, use the mix of herbs I'd meticulously gathered to block anyone else from finding their scent, and prepare myself for a trip to Hell. The shadow portal at the alter sometimes opens on its own, but I couldn't wait for that.

Only gods, goddesses, and those with a gift from either could open a portal. I was none of the above so I shouldn't be able to do it. I never had before being imprisoned here. In fact, I never had until a little more than a quarter century ago.

When Taryn had been reincarnated into this new life.

Everything was different this time. All four of us knew it. I was just the only one who had the guts to defy our duty and do what had to be done with this last chance.

I pushed away the dark stain on my soul and pulled upon her power. The light from her magic, bubbled up inside of me and I opened my hand. The darkness of the shadow pooled like a cauldron being stirred, opening wider and wider, until the fires of Hell flickered through, lighting up the burned out shell of the church.

Sometimes when other portals were open, I could see through them like an eyeglass telescope. I suspected this was how Father Joachim predicted Taryn's arrival, and not some mystical precognition or message from God.

At least this time, there were no demon dragon wyrms or the God of Chaos to fight off. Which must mean they were busy. If anyone could survive a trip to Hell, it was August and Vas. But the sooner I got the two of them out of there, the better.

Then I was going to throw their dumb asses into my dungeon too.

I take several deep breaths of the cool Siberian night air, shift into my more powerful wolf form, then dive into the portal. The heat hits me right in the face. No amount of panting is going to cool me down. I never thought I'd appreciate eternal winter, but fuck. I'm wishing for snow right now.

The first thing I do is reach out through our pack connection. *August, Vas, tell me where you are.*

No response. I don't even feel the touch of their minds. Yet somehow I also know they aren't dead. They're here, but something is blocking us from communicating. I know only a little about the Queen of the Underworld and her powers, but her consort, Nergal doesn't have the ability to do this.

One more item on my to do list while I'm in Hell. Find out why the rulers of the underworld are interested in Taryn, and why they're working with the Volkovs. Even for Rasputin, this was a dangerous game.

The maze of tunnels carved out of the sharp and craggily rock is endless. I open my senses as wide as I can, searching for any sign of my fellow guardsmen. Their scents are nowhere near, but I catch a faint whiff of something other than demons and brimstone ahead. That's the only clue I have, so that's where I'll start.

I give one last glance at the portal, hold up my paw and let the magic flow to close it. I can't risk leaving it open for any wyrm to come upon. Not if I'm not there to protect the island. My tether back is Taryn. As long as she lives, I will always have a way to get home.

Because she has always been and will always be my home. No matter what century, what continent, what life, she is mine.

It's no use trying to hide in the shadows when the demons can appear out of even the smallest sliver of it. I stalk down the tunnel where the different scent is the strongest, keeping ultra alert for signs of August and Vas, or danger.

What I find is neither.

Dragging a sword as tall as she is, and a belt full of daggers, the little girl we met the last time I was thrown into Hell, trots down the corridor as if this is nothing more than a school hallway. I still don't understand what the fuck a human girl is doing in Hell. She shouldn't have been able to survive even a moment, much less be walking around like this is her personal playground.

She spots me and hauls her sword up in front of her, and points the tip right at me. "No, puppy. Bad. Go home. Go home, right now."

I don't move an inch. I have no idea what kind of a creature she is. She definitely human, but more. What I do catch is the distinct scent of wolves. She isn't one, but she's been near them.

The little girl sighs, rolls her eyes at me, and drops the

tip of the sword into the dirt. I almost laugh because she's so very clearly irritated that I am causing her some kind of inconvenience by not doing as I'm told. If I had robes and could shift so that I wasn't a large naked male, I'd do so and ask her who she is and what she's doing down here. Since that isn't happening, I can't waste anymore time. She may be the key to finding August and Vas.

When I rescue them from these depths, we can bring her back to Fire Island with us. She'd eternally be the same age, but being six-ish years old for a lifetime has to be better than growing up in Hell.

Slowly and carefully I approach her, with my head slung low, so she knows I'm not a threat. I'm twice as big as she is, but she seems completely unafraid. Her scent is strange, like nothing else I've smelled either. It's almost like a dragon. But there is no such thing as female dragons. I don't smell the telltale bitterness of fear or aggression from her. She won't attack me. Not that I think she could do much damage with a sword she can barely lift.

She watches me with narrowed eyes, but when I put my snout into her hand to show her I mean her no harm. She sighs again like she's put out. "Dumb puppy. Come on."

With a tug of the fur at the scruff of my neck, she leads me deeper into the depths of the tunnels. It's clear she knows exactly where she's going and I have to pay a lot of attention to make sure I can get back. The thing keeping me by her side is that faint scent of wolf on her.

I can't tell if it's August or Vas. There are simply too

many other scents surrounding her and I can't pick out any one in particular. Who or what is this child?

She holds her fingers up to her lips to signal that I should be silent. It's not like I'm going to run around howling or anything, but I nod my understanding anyway. Together we creep up to a crossroads of tunnels and I can hear a horde of demon dragon wyrms nearby.

"Bad demons," she whispers and points around the corner. The way she says it makes me think that there are good demons too. Uh. I didn't realize there was any other kind.

She darts across the opening to a different tunnel and waves to me to follow. I can't help but glance to where the dumb demons are gathered. Even that short glimpse turns my stomach. The Black Dragon of Hell is fucking some other kind of demon I've never seen before.

That is something a little girl shouldn't see. I hurry across the gap and give her a little shove forward. She takes several steps, then turns and smacks me on the nose. "Don't touch. Ouch."

She curls in on herself and puts a hand on one of her daggers. I take a step back and sit, trying again to make myself less threatening. She's injured somehow, but doesn't want me to see her pain.

My heart pounds in my chest like a battle axe cutting open my chest. This child reminds me so much of Taryn with her fierce bravery. If I didn't know Taryn was in my dungeon and not awaiting reincarnation, I'd think this is where she went between each life, that this was her.

A moment later, she pulls the dagger from the belt at her waist and holds it out in front of her. "Jett."

She says this name as if she was swearing. There is no fear in her. Again, more like frustration. I move to get in front of her, the need to protect her just as strong as with Taryn. Whoever this girl is, she's important to the world.

Another horde of demon wyrms trample down the tunnel towards us. I growl and prepare to rip these demons apart, but just before they are within striking distance, the largest of the demons stops. It hisses at me but doesn't move any closer. I recognize it as the same one she protected us from before.

The little girl crawls underneath me and pops up between my legs. "Puppies not yours. Go away." She sticks out her tongue at the demon wyrm and points her dagger at its face.

The demon hisses again and the way they react to each other reminds me of the Romanov siblings. Always bickering, but they cared for each other. I don't see how a demon and a girl of unknown species could be related. Then the demon spoke. It actually said real words and pointed at me. "Fallyn have two. Jett want one."

Hell was getting stranger and stranger by the minute. The girl, Fallyn, has two puppies. That had to be August and Vas. Thank the Goddess.

Fallyn stomped her foot. "No. Puppies leave."

"Jett leave Hell," the beast shouts. He directs his next words at me. "Wolf take Jett to portal or wolf die."

TARYN

*I*t doesn't occur to me until what felt like hours later, that my magic could probably help Father Joachim heal. Duh. I already knew that the shifters heal faster when they were in their animal forms. I still didn't really think of myself as one of them, I realize.

My own shift was different. Their skin split and their bones cracked when they went from one form to another. My magic just sort of made me into a wolf. I wonder if I can shift into other animals too. Or for that matter, other forms all together. Like can I become foggy like the Nothing? That was something I would try after Father Joachim was awake.

I rest my hand on his back, right between his shoulder bones and close my eyes. Wait. Why was I always doing that? It's not as if I need total darkness to call the magic up or something. In fact, everything worked better when there was light. Specifically moonlight.

Whatever I am, human, wolf, witch, something else, I think the wolves Goddess of the Moon had maybe bestowed this magic on me. I'd felt something stir inside of me when Alida was telling the story of how she'd given their people the ability to defend themselves.

I wish I'd had more time to hear more and ask questions. But I absolutely didn't regret getting busy with Vas and August instead. But if my powers also came from her, why didn't she just make me a wolf shifter too? What makes me so special?

I promise myself, sitting here in the dark, that I will find out who this Goddess is and why she chose me to have this magic. I suspect she also has a hand in matching me up with my wolves. There's so much more to the feelings I have for them, even the Dark Prince, than simply attraction. Even love doesn't feel like a strong enough word.

It's that feeling that I draw upon to pull the magic up now and try to heal Father Joachim. I watch very closely as my hand begins to glow. I bring up the memories of him comforting me with his soft wisdom when we first met and I was still so lost as to who, where, and why I was here.

He doesn't move and nothing changes. I need to do more. The instant attraction to him is a pretty damn strong emotion, so I let that bubble up next. The light in the room increases, and not just my fingers are glowing now, but my whole arm.

Vas taught me that the most instinctual base emotions are what I should use to control the shift, and I guess it's the same with this magic too. What's more instinctual than sex?

I reach out to Father Joachim with my mind, even though I don't think he can hear me. I push the memories of how much I wanted him when I mated with August. The way he touched himself because he couldn't help it turned me on so much.

He stirs, just the slightest movement in his legs, as if he's really only a big dog having a dream. It's working so I pull up the next memory. This time he's pressing his cock to my lips, letting his orgasm overwhelm him and me. I felt so happy and guilty at the same time that I wanted him to let me taste him, but knowing he thought it was wrong.

What I wouldn't give to see him lose all control.

Our entire side of the room is glowing with my magic and something is definitely happening to Father Joachim. He's breathing is better and he doesn't seem to be in as much pain as before, but he's still unconscious. I need to give him more, but I'm fresh out of memories.

Well, here goes nothing. In my mind's eye I imagine what I really want to do with Father Joachim. I want him bared to me, not just his body but his soul. No more secrets, no lies. He'll bite my neck and mark me, and he won't feel guilt, but the same pleasure that I do. Then with August, Vasily, and even the Dark Prince as our witnesses, I want him to claim me.

As I think about this scenario, I can literally feel the magic doing what I want. Father Joachim's internal bleeding slows, then stops, and the injuries knit themselves back together. His broken bones mend, and I sense the moment he becomes conscious again.

Out of the corner of my eye I see his prayer beads, nestled in the pile of robes he dropped when he shifted to fight the Nothing. They're glowing with the same blue light of my magic. I always assumed Father was an ordained priest of the Russian Orthodox church. But what if his religion is that of this Goddess of the Moon? That makes a heck of a lot more sense.

He does talk of God, but also of the Goddess. He's the one I understand the least about. So far I have no past memories of him, but there is a very distinct sense that his vows to Christianity are comforting to me, but that a religion that stems from the mythology of wolf-shifters and the moon is also right for both of us.

"Father Joachim, can you hear me? Are you all right now?" I gave him one last push of magic and he shifts from wolf to man. At least I know how to do that one thing right.

His back is to me and he slowly rolls over to face me. He has that same kind of dazed look as when I made him shift from wolf to man the other time. When I remove my hand and let the magic recede back inside of me, he gets more alert pretty fast.

"Taryn? I'm the one that should be asking if you're alright. I'm supposed to protect you, not the other way around." He sits up and scrubs his hand over his face and looks around. "Grigori always did like a secret dungeon to punish those that would harm you."

In just those two or three sentences, Father Joachim has revealed more about who and what he and the Dark Prince are to me than the entire rest of the time I've been with them on this island. Maybe I should use more magic on him to make him spill all his secrets.

I get a yucky indigestion rumble in my stomach from even the thought of using my power to manipulate him. Vas said I had to discover who and what I am for myself, that they couldn't tell me. I want to trust in my wolves, that they know best. They certainly all remember more than I do.

Father Joachim grabs his robes and his prayer beads. The beads, he wraps around his wrist securing them with a quick loop and a twist. He shoves the robes through the bars to me. "Put these on, *boginya*. You shouldn't be subjected to such cold.

I'd rather he and I snuggled for warmth, but I suppose the bars would make that hard. Besides, if I put on his robes, Father Joachim can't hide himself from me. Gah. I know I shouldn't be thinking about anything but escape, but the attraction I have to him just takes over my brain sometimes.

Besides the fact that I've just spent the last few minutes imagining all the deliciously dirty things we have done and could be doing together. I'm so going to hell.

Why do I have sex on the brain when I should just be working on getting out of here and avenging August and Vas? I'm blaming the Dark Prince and that red hot kiss.

Okay, time to get my mind out of the freaking gutter...dungeon...whatever, and get back to the plan.

I slip into the robes, and the scent of Father Joachim send all the tingles to all the places I want him to touch me. Later, body. Geez, get a grip. "Father, can you get out of your cell? I'm locked in tight."

He looks around, and examines the bars. "Does the demon who pushed me into the cell appear often? Is it guarding you?"

"The Nothing? I didn't realize it was a demon." That would mean, what? The Nothing had eaten me and I'd been living inside of it, then it puked me onto the island. Horrifying. "The only other time I've seen it was before I came here."

"The Nothing is a good name for the shadow. But it is merely the element the demons use to travel. There was also a demon here, that came from that cell over there. That's what I fought against."

"The only other thing down here is Peter, and he's mostly dead." I pointed in the direction of Peter's putrid smell.

"*Demon, ty govorish' cherez Pyotr Fyodorovicha?*"

Uh, that's interesting. I don't understand how or why, but I know that Father Joachim is speaking Russian and that he asked if the demon was speaking through Peter. When I first landed on the island Peter had spoken several other languages to me and I hadn't understood them at all. This had to be a side effect of the Goddess's magic, but what a strange one.

Or was it because more of my past life memories were manifesting and I'd lived so many of them in Russia that the language was latent in my mind?

Something moves in Peter's cell. I squint to see, but it was still so dark. I call up my wolf trying to focus on only shifting my eyes to use the better vision. Slowly the shapes in the room became more clear and a very raggedy looking Peter, his head lolling to the side and his limbs at weird angles was standing behind the bars. Eek.

"Why do you think I'm possessed by a demon, priest?"

I grab Father Joachim's hand through the bars. Whatever that is on the other side of the room, it is not a person. If the creepy crawlies of disgust feels like bugs crawling through sludge dripping down your insides, then I am infested with both heebies and jeebies, because eww. The sight and sound of the demon coming out of Peter is beyond disturbing.

"Because Peter is clearly dead, but his body has not been taken by the island and his soul has not been claimed by the Goddess, as is her right with all her people." Joachim's tone was calm and even as if he is having a conversation with any Joe Schmoe.

"Your Goddess has forsaken her people. Or have you not noticed?" Peterdemon's arm flings around as if he is trying to indicate the dire circumstances we're in, but instead he just looks like a marionette doll that the puppeteer doesn't have much practice using.

"Your mind tricks won't work on me." Father Joachim waves the demon's threat away.

I cover a snort because I almost said - These are not the droids you're looking for - out loud. It is so weird how my memories come back to me in these little blips. It never seems to be the important ones, always just tiny slices of my life. But I do know now I had a bit of a crush on young Obi Wan Kenobi. Which explains a lot.

Father Joachim gives my hand a little squeeze and continues to chastise Peterdemon. "I am not your average priest. My connection to the Goddess is stronger than you can imagine. Now, tell me your name so I can banish you and be done with your insolence."

The Father's confidence and bravado with this creepy beast is delicious. It makes me want to jump his bones even more. It also gives me a bit of bravery. I bet if my magic repelled the Nothing, the shadow, that this demon hid in, I can help banish the actual demon too.

"Yeah. I want you gone, Darth Creepo. Go back to where you came from." I point at Peterdemon and give a little wiggle of my fingers. Father Joachim grabs my hand, covering it with his fist so fast, I didn't even get one sparkle of magic out.

I give him a what-the-literal-hell, but don't say anything because his eyes are wide and he's giving me the same look back. "Don't let him see what you can do, *sladkaya boginya.* It is my duty to protect you from Hell's beasts."

"But I want to help. I can do it."

"You can. Why do you think he did not attack you already? But I have failed you for so long, allow me to do my duty."

Peterdemon shakes the bars and the shadow bubbles up around his feet. "You can not hide her from me any longer, priest. She will be forever vulnerable in the darkness without her guards. I have three and your soul is already tainted by my realm. Give her to me."

I rip my hand from Father Joachim's hold, rush the bars of my cage and shoot a beam of magic at this pile of poo. My light grabs him up just as it did my wolves at the beach. But this time through the connection, I can feel the chaos and darkness that embodies this beast of Hell. "Are you saying you have August, Vasily, and the Dark Prince imprisoned in Hell?"

Peterdemon flails and squeaks. Father Joachim joins me at the door to our cells and clears his throat. "I guess we're doing this your way. Fine. The demon speaks through Peter and you're crushing his windpipe. He cannot answer."

"Oh. Does it hurt the demon when I do it?"

"I think not."

"Too bad." I concentrate and lesson my magical hold. "Now, talk you shitstick."

His voice comes out raspy and broken, but darker and more menacing than before. Whatever remnant of Peter may have remained, it's gone now and only the beast from Hell remains. "Choke me harder, mommy."

I'm sure that is supposed to shock me, but I've got no fucks left to give with this guy. "My pleasure."

I narrow my eyes and clench my fingers around the magic as if it's actually the demon's throat. Peterdemon gurgles and scratches at his throat as if he can pull my fingers away. He can't. Ha. He doesn't like this and I do think it hurts him. I relent a little and ask again, "Do you have my Wolf Guard imprisoned in Hell?"

"No," he says and cough laugh.

Father Joachim crosses his arms. "He's deflecting. Ask him in a different way."

I think Father Joachim has done this kind of thing before. Have I done it with him? "Do you know where August, Vasily, and the Dark Prince are?"

"Yes. They're in my domain. You can't touch them in Hell, or you'll face my wrath."

Father gives his wrist a shake. "Hell is not yours though, is it. It's Ereshkigal's. Does she know the chaos you're wreaking on the mortal plane, Nergal."

Nergal? This super evil demon from Hell's name is Nergal? Worst villain name ever. He apparently doesn't like it either because he screams and writhes around like a rodent caught on a fishing line.

"Quickly, sweet light, while you've still got him in your hold, demand he bring them back from Hell to you. Your power over him will compel him to do as you say."

It will? Badass. "I want my Guard back, Nergally Wergally. Bring me the Dark Prince, Aug—"

Before I could get out August and Vasily's names, Peter-demon's body goes slack and all the shadow bubbling around the dungeon fades away like fog in the early morning sun. I pull my magic back and drop the body of the thing that used to be a man to the floor.

The light in the room dims back to the near complete darkness. I like this new hold on the powers inside of me. The first lesson I learned when I got to this island was one of love. But the second one was that I am powerful. I forgot that.

I won't again.

GRIGORI

*I*f not for the little girl, I would have probably just ripped this talking demon dragon to shreds. I'd take my chances with the rest of his brethren. But I couldn't do that if it would put her in danger.

I'm not shifting out of my powerful wolf to my more vulnerable human form just to have a chat. I have shit to do and none of it involves parlaying with minions from Hell. I could run the other way and hope to catch August and Vas's scent, or I could stay and fight.

I didn't like either option. What I need is more info from the little girl on where my fellow guards are, not a fight.

Fuck. I was going to have to shift.

I growl and snap at the demon wyrm and it backs off a bit. As the magic of the shift rolls through me, I stay in a position low to the ground, squatting, to be able to protect my stomach and groin areas. Not to mention, I'm not walking around naked in front of a child.

The moment I'm in my human form, the girl claps and smiles at me. "Good job, puppy. My turn."

A different kind of magic than what I'm used to seeing rolls across the little girl and before my eyes, she goes from six to something like twenty. Her hair looks like it's made of flames, and the once heavy sword looks much more deadly hanging from her belt along with a dozen or so daggers.

The demon wyrm doesn't seem bothered by the fact that she's become and adult in the blink of an eye, leaving me to believe that this is not the first time she's done this. A disguise she uses, perhaps? "Do you know where the other wolves sucked down into Hell are, Fallyn?"

The demon wyrm moves closer. "I know. You show portal. I show wolves."

Fallyn smacks the demon on the nose just as she did me. "My turn, I said."

The demon wyrm pouts, like actually scowls and looks hurt but doesn't do anything more than sit back and wait for Fallyn to have her turn. She looks at me again and says, "Izzy said I should help your moon, because her children are going to be important later. Do you know the babies?"

What? "I don't have children, and who is Izzy?"

She rolled her eyes at me like I was stupid, but then turns and clearly hears something the rest of us can't. "He's coming. Hurry. I will help you, you help Jett, Jett will find the unicorn, she will help the dragons, and then I can help the mermaid's children, and they can help the sacrifice and the savior, and..."

I understand the individual words coming out of her mouth, but not when they were strung together in some kind of fairy story. Whatever kind of creature this Fallyn is, she's been in Hell too long, and I want to make sure she gets out of here with me. "Yes, I will help Jett."

Was I lying? A little bit. If Jett the demon dragon wanted to get out of Hell, as long as he didn't come to terrorize the island, fine. I wasn't sure how to help him. It's not as if he could borrow magic from the Goddess to open a shadow portal. But I would certainly show him how I did it and fulfill my end of the bargain.

"Where are the other wolves?"

The ceiling of rock above us rattled and small stones shook loose falling down on us. Fallyn and Jett looked at each other with worry in their eyes. Fallyn wrinkled her nose. "Uh-oh. You run, I go hide with the puppies. Come back later."

"No, I need to take the wolves back with me now. We don't need to run and hide, we can fight." If no one else had ever defended this woman besides herself, I would. No way I was letting another special woman die on my watch.

I shift back into my wolf form and push my senses out to pinpoint the threat. The ground around us shakes even more and a shadow portal opens above our heads not more than a few feet away. Many of the demon wyrms who'd had Jett's back when he was ready to attack me, bolt away in fear.

The portal warps and gyrates like no other I'd ever seen. Out of the darkness, the God of Chaos, half man-half owl, like a winged demon of death, drops to the dirt. This is no power move by Nergal. He isn't attacking, he's been attacked.

If he's been back to Fire Island again, while I was down here and couldn't defend Taryn, there's no telling what kind of havoc he's wrought. Father Joachim seems to have done his job though, because Nergal is looking like shit. What I don't understand is his interest in Taryn. He hasn't bothered with her or our people in thousands of years. Not since his attacks so long ago that prompted the Goddess to give us our shifting abilities in the first place. Why now?

I'll just have to kick his ass and find out.

To his credit, Jett moves next to me, pushing Fallyn behind us both. But she is the one who strikes first. One of her daggers flies through the air over my head, striking not Nergal, but the unstable rocks above him where the misshapen portal had been. A landslide of stone falls down on him, blocking my path back to where I need to go to open the portal back to the church.

"Now we run and hide." Fallyn grabs me by the scruff of the neck and slaps a hand against the wall. Trails of sparkling fire magic drop from the ceiling and reveal a dozen small caves that were previously hidden. I've lived long enough to see the rise of elemental magic and realize, the girl is some kind of a fire witch. Although, she's using magic in a way I've never seen or heard of.

She drags me toward one of the caves and as we pass

through her curtain of magic, I feel a zip like lightning in the air. I can see out, but the way the demon wyrms are looking around, they can't see in. Inside is more weapons in various states of disrepair and the distinct scent of August and Vas. But they aren't here.

Outside Nergal has broken out of the pile of rock and is advancing on Jett and his fellows that did not flee. I won't have them sacrificing themselves while I stand here in relative safety, but I also can't let that beast get anywhere near Fallyn. I sniff around the cave loudly doing my best to show her that I want to know where the other wolves are.

She's very clever and shakes her head and holds her finger to her lips. "Not here. Sleeping, shhh."

The sounds outside the cave are muted, but I think she's trying to tell me they can still hear us. Likely as much as we can hear them. We're safe for the moment, but won't be for much longer.

Nergal is advancing and he swipes at one of the demon wyrms. It goes flying and smacks against the nearest wall. Jett goes berserk and runs forward on the attack. Right behind him, from the darkness, two huge wolves bound into the fray.

August and Vasily.

They're looking a little worse for their time in Hell, singed fur, dirty muzzles, unhealed cuts and scrapes. But their healthy enough to fight, and the pins and needles of worry I've felt for them dissipates. Taryn's the one who has been worried about them, not me. She needs them. I don't need anyone.

I lower my head and growl as August and Vas coordinate their attack on Nergal. They won't be able to defeat or kill the God, but we can incapacitate him and keep him from attacking long enough to escape.

"No, puppy. Shh." Fallyn holds her daggers at the ready, but she doesn't want Nergal to see her. I don't blame her. She's safe here in her cave, but I can't stay while other fight for us. Gently I place my head against her shoulder and back her up to the farthest wall of the cave, then stare at her unmoving, willing her to understand that she mustn't move.

She nods and while I doubt she'll hear or understand, I tell her what I wish I'd said to Taryn so many times over the years. *You're strong,* oomnyashka. *You don't need anyone to save you or protect you.*

My sweet fierce Taryn. It was my duty to protect her, but she always had the power to do it herself. Even before the Goddess made her the Queen of Wolves and touched her with the magical power of the moon.

I shake off the memories. Nothing better to distract myself than a good old fashioned brawl between good and evil. That same zip of fire magic passes through me when I go through Fallyn's hidden barrier. I've got the element of surprise and I'm taking full advantage of it.

With one big leap, I rebound off the wall and over the heads of most of the demons. The momentum from my push off the wall propels me straight into Nergal's chest. He falls backward, because he'd been bracing himself for a head on attack by August, Vas, and the demon dragons. Surprise, asshole.

Well, well, look who finally showed up to the fight. August blasts forward, rushing past me to land on one of the demon's wings, and Vas is right behind to pin the other one to the ground.

The scent of irritation, anger, and disappointment waft off Vasily so strongly that I don't have to guess what he's thinking right now. *If you're here, who is protecting the princess?*

Your sacrifice was not for nothing. She is safe. Joachim is with her. He doesn't need to know that they are both imprisoned, only that they are together and Taryn is out of harms way. Soon the two of them will be too and I can finally rest.

I follow Vas and August's defense strategy and charge forward to land directly on Nergal's chest, pinning him to the ground. Since he is a God and I am an alpha, he can hear me though mindspeak. *What is your interest in Taryn?*

It's not like I expected him to answer. It seemed like he had beef with August and Vas and I'd bet they'd been tracking him while down here, and not the other way around. I'd expect no less from elite warriors I'd trained. Even if Nergal did nothing but squawk, I'd bet the two of them had some intel on Hell's plans.

This asshole thrashes around like a bird caught in a trap, and it surprises me that he hasn't yet thrown us off. Perhaps when we battled him in our realm we weakened him, because there was no way this was his full strength. He wasn't mentally in the game either.

My end game is supposed to be to get August and Vas out of Hell, and rescue Tar...uh Fallyn. Fucking around with the God of Chaos wasn't getting that done. I swipe a claw across one of his wings and he thrashes about, throwing August and Vas.

Get to the tunnel where the portal back to the church is. I'll be right behind you to open it.

Both of them hesitate, but then take off running. The demon wyrms are closing in, and I think they'd like to take advantage of the weakened position Nergal is in. I'll happily let them chomp on him.

I jump away and they move in. None of us are fast enough. The demon beast snatches one of the wyrms and rips its throat out with his teeth, drinking down the beasts blood. Jett makes an unholy war cry and the room explodes into battle. Demon wyrms are attacking and being attacked if Nergal was dazed from where ever he crashed in from, he's got his wits back now.

And he's pissed.

At me.

I'd intended to grab Fallyn and slip away during the fight, but if I even attempted to get close to her, I'd be exposing her. I'll be back for her, I swear it. I turn and run down the tunnel after August and Vas. They have to be my first priority.

I owe a debt to Fallyn and Jett that I must find a way to repay, but not now. I don't get more than a few leaps into the darkness, when I hear Nergal screech and in an instant he's flying over my head. His great claws dig into my fur and the muscles on my back, snatching me up into the air. He slams me into the wall and lands in front of me, talons extended, going for my throat.

I dodge, but he catches me on the chest instead, ripping me open all the way to the bone. Fuck that hurts. This wound is deep enough that even my wolf was going to have a hard time healing this wound. I slide down the wall and all I can do now is pray.

My hubris has screwed us all. Because while I marked Taryn, I did not claim her, we did not mate, and without that bond, she cannot ascend as the Queen of the Wolves. I pray hard to the Goddess who gave me the responsibility to keep my Queen safe to spare me this one last time. If I die, here in Hell, I pray that she brings me back to life and shows me the way to find Taryn once again.

I pray.

But there is no answer.

Only Hell.

Nergal grabs me again and lifts me up by the scruff of my neck. "Your Goddess sent me for you. But she didn't say I had to send you back alive. Death is so much more fun."

The last of my life's blood trickles down through my fur and the world around me is fading to black. I barely understand the words the God of Chaos hisses. The Goddess wants me. That's all I get.

Nergal plucks a feather from his arm and slaps it against my chest. "Give her this for me."

A shadow portal opens above me and I can see through all of space and time. My queen is waiting for me, and I want nothing more than to go to her. I'm not even bothered when Nergal squeezes my throat, choking the last of my breath from me.

In my very last moment of consciousness, I see a dagger, alight with the flames of fire magic fly through the air and strike Nergal's feathered head right in the temple. His feathers burst into flames and he screams out, dropping me into the portal and clawing at the dagger and flames.

I fall into the darkness of the shadow, into nothing, and I die.

TARYN

Something has changed and I don't like it. Everything feels wrong, like a piece of me has fallen off and gone missing. I gasp at the wrenching in my chest and clasp Father Joachim's hand harder. "Do you feel it too?"

He nods gravely. I think he knows what's happening but before I can ask him, a portal opens up right where that demon vanished into the dirt and a body so bloody and torn he's unrecognizable crashes into the room. Oh no. Oh no no no no no.

It's the Dark Prince of Wolves. And I think he's dead.

Did I do this? When I told that vile demon to bring him back to me, I set a dangerous being on him. Now he's suffered the consequences of having me in his life just like August and Vasily did. I scooch away from Father Joachim. If I'm not careful, he'll be next and I need him to not be. He's my last life line, the only thing keeping me sane.

I can't lose the Dark Prince, August, and Vasily. I can't.

I can't breathe.

I can't think.

Little spots are swirling through my vision. One second I'm a badass demon shit-talker and the next I'm a pile of cortisol.

"You're going to be okay, Taryn. Breathe." Father Joachim's calm voice filters in to my full on panic attack.

"N-no. I won't. It's too much, Father. I'm not strong enough to handle all the death and despair of this island, this prison. I want to go home." I've never said that out loud before. I don't even know where home is, but I know I had one. Anything is better than the constant threats and killing.

Words pop into my head that I don't want to hear right now. *You're strong. You don't need anyone to save you or protect you.*

Tears form, blotting out the little vision I have in this darkness. They pool, but don't fall. Why is that the one thing I needed to hear? It pools in my heart and I blink, letting the tears fall just so I can wipe them from my face. From the moment I was thrown out of the Nothing and onto this island, I've let everyone else take care of me.

I wanted their protection.

But did I need it?

I've made a lot of mistakes in the short amount of time I've been here. I'm sure I made mistakes before this, in my life outside the prison that I've only started to remember. It's probably what got me thrown in here in the first place.

But these words, telling me that I am enough, they mean everything to me.

I take a shaky breath and push the sentiment deep into my heart. I'm sure I'll screw up again, but it's even worse if I fall apart and lose all hope. Nope. No. No way.

There is always hope. I'm done with these rollercoaster emotions. Either I've got the grit, determination and hope inside of me to survive or I don't.

And I know that I do. It's scary to even think about letting it all out, becoming who I'm meant to be, but I have to, because continuing to react to everything that happens to me feels to much like I'm a victim and that's never what I want for myself. I'm better than that, God dammit.

Okay, so what do I do now? I'm done freaking out, and I need to deal with this situation. Which is a dead mate out of reach, two more somewhere in Hell, and another one mentally out of reach on the other side of these bars. Yes, I was now 100% sure that all four were absolutely mine. They belong to me, and my heart to them.

It's time I did something about that instead of idly waiting for them to save me and make me stronger. I blow out a long breath and turn to Father Joachim. He's not going to like my plan, but I must convince him it's the only way.

I consider a million different ways to ask for what I need, but in the end, I just blurt it out. "You need to bite me, give me your mate mark."

Father Joachim jerks back like I'd slapped him. "Taryn, I can't. I vowed that--"

I hold up a hand to stop that line of discussion. "You don't have to have sex with me. I know you don't want to, and I swear I won't push you beyond this. But I know that we belong to each other just as I do with August and Vasily. The same as with the Dark Prince. I can't let him just die, and I can't let you deny what we both want and need any longer."

Father Joachim bows his head and I think that he's praying, probably for the strength to resist temptation. I want to respect his beliefs, but I want a real life more, and I want it with him, with all of my wolves. That means I'll do whatever I can to save the prince.

I know I have power in me and that it can heal, but I also know there's a lot more potential than the little bit I've discovered in myself. Every time I bond with one of my mates, I get more glimpses of my past lives, and more access to power.

I've been marked by three. Something inside of me knows that completing that circle will open up this power inside of me. If I can heal, maybe I can also bring someone back from the dead.

The voice that told me I am strong was his voice. There is still a spark of life in him, I can feel it. We can't wait a whole lot longer though. "Please, Father Joachim."

He slowly raises his face and looks me in the eye. There isn't pain, or reticence, or even anger there. There's fear. He's afraid, and I didn't think that was possible. He's always the calm and confident one with all the answers. I've seen him fight, literally tooth and claw, and he's so centered that I didn't even think fear was in his emotional wheel house.

But he's scared, and I think it's of me. Well, shit. Add that to the list of things I need to figure out and resolve.

He fingers the prayer beads that are his ever present companion. They glow with the same light as my magic again and I realize for they were a gift from the Goddess. They are his comfort. "I am yours, Taryn. I have been and always will be. I want only to do what is best for you. If you need me to break these vows for you... I will do my best to live with the consequences."

My heart fills with overwhelming joy and breaks at the same time. I don't want his love, his mind, body, and soul out of obligation. But right now, in this moment, for today, I will take this as a step forward. Not a win, but the move in the right direction.

"I don't know what to say, except thank you." That doesn't come out sounding the way it did in my head. This isn't some cold transaction, and I don't like the clammy swirl in my chest. "I'm sorry."

"No, *boginya*. I am the one who should apologize to you. I hope someday I will get the chance to do that. Until then, we will make the best of what we have to do. Come, let me fulfill your simple request."

This is anything but simple. I didn't want this intimate act to feel like a transaction and now it's all awkward and weird. I can't let that stop me. Whenever I figure out what in the world is going on in Father Joachim's head, I'll get him to reveal the secrets that are keeping us apart. Because it has to be more than a vow to a religion.

Until then, I'm going to try to make this as good for him as I know it will be for me. This isn't my first marking rodeo. I've imagined what it would be like to be held in his arms, for him to kiss me with all the passion burning inside of him, and to mark me. More than that, I want him to take me, just as August and Vasily have.

I'm imagining what that would be like right now, and Father Joachim groans. Is he scenting my arousal, my desire for him, or can he hear my thoughts like the others? I can feel the connection between us bringing the magic up inside of me already.

I'd love to take our time, to seduce him, entice him, make him forget all about these other vows. But I can feel the spark of life in the Dark Prince sputtering, reaching out for the bit of magic too. I want them both, but can't have them both at the same time. Not while one doesn't want me and the other one is dying.

I have to take what I need from Father Joachim and help the prince. Then I'm digging into him hard to find out what's keeping us apart. With that resolve in my mind, I move to the bars between the two of us with my arms open.

The fear is still banked in his eyes, but I can see that he's trying. He understands what's at stake here.

"Will you kiss me first? I understand if that's too much, but I'd like it." And I think he would too.

"*Boginya*, I want very little more than that, but I think

it's best if we do this quickly. I can sense the power in you reaching out, ready to heal Grigori, just as you did me. If he can be saved, only you can do it."

See? Awkward. But fine. I'll deal with that later. "Okay. Bite me."

Did I say that with a little too much snark? Yes. Did I still mean it? Also yes. I really, really wanted him to bite me and bite me hard. In fact I was really giddy inside. Like my magic is turning into butterflies on crack in my lower belly.

Both of us press our bodies against the bars between us. Never did I imagine I'd ever be trying to get busy in an actual jail. What is this the Old West? Ooh, just the anticipation of having Father Joachim's lips on my skin, his teeth digging into my flesh is bringing up memories.

I'm so close to breaking through the mental barriers that the Nothing placed in my mind, that I can almost reach out and touch them. What I do in reality is reach out and touch Father Joachim. I cup his cheek and slowly caress my way down his throat. He swallows and his breathing goes shallow and raspy like he's trying not to let me see him sweat.

"Kiss me. Let me have just a little of what you don't want me to have." I lick my lips, imagining his on mine.

Why is it so deliciously sensual to be with him? I already know he's mine, and I assume we've been together, like in all the ways two souls can be intertwined. I know I'm asking for something he doesn't want to give. Except he does, I could never even ask if I thought he truly didn't want me.

"I do want it, I simply can't." He leans into my touch. "You are more tempting to me than you could ever know."

He runs his lips softly across my cheek, from nose to temple, in a kiss so light it sends shivers across my skin.

I guess I'm asking for something he isn't supposed to give, and that rebellion, against everything in this life, and possibly all my past lives, is thrilling. No more will I cower and take what's been thrown at me. Yet I also cannot force myself on this kind, gentle warrior.

Again, I tell him that I'm sorry. Not with words, but with my heart. He whispers my heart's sentiments back to me. "I wish I could give you more. I'm sorry."

He buries his face in the crook of my neck, and scrapes his teeth across the skin there. Magic and lust rush up through every cell in my body and I reach through the bars and clasp his head, holding him to me. As he sinks his teeth into me, all the need for him that I've tried to hold back explodes through me.

I go from zero to orgasm in less than a moment and cry out with the nirvana of it all. The magic inside of me flows out in crashing waves, filling the room with light and warmth. The bars between us melt away, and I slip the robes off my shoulders and arms so I can be that much closer to him.

It isn't only magic and lust that crashes into me. I'm flooded with memories and power. I see flashes of our past lives together, and how he has always been the wise council for not only the rest of the Wolf Guard, but for me as well. We've always shared the love of knowing there is something greater in the universe than we.

In more lives than not, we have both turned to religion, even though it doesn't quite hold the everything we need to believe in. No wonder he's made vows to a God that can't be broken. He's done that for me.

Before either of us are done reveling in each other, I pull away. I've taken more than I should from him. "Forgive me, Father."

I have sinned.

Against him.

But I would do it again, and I'm not sorry.

Father Joachim steps back, bows his head, and covers his groin with his hands, in a way that's less hiding his erection from me, and more genuflecting. I'll let him be for now because I've gotten all that he promised he could give me.

The room around us is still bathed in my magic's blue sparkling light. The jail cell bars between all three of us are nothing more than stalactites and stalagmites of melted metal. I touch his cheek one last time and step around the debris left in the wake of my newfound power.

The magic is growing inside of me this time, not fading away. The more Joachim's mark on my skin takes on it's final form, the stronger I feel. There will be no more hiding in the shadows and darkness. This light is mine and it's never going out.

I cross to the broken body of Grigori, my Dark Prince, and reach for the spark of life in him. When I press my hand against his chest, hot, blue light surrounds him and the great tear in his skin and bones knits back together. He gasps and his back bows, the life in him reawakening. For one shining moment, he opens his eyes and looks at me, not with the anger and disdain of before, but with the love in his broken heart.

I can heal his wounds, but it will take more than magic to heal his heart.

JOACHIM

What have I done? Oh Goddess, what have I done?

I shake my bowed head and swallow back the gut-wrenching spasms, the bile rising up my throat, the mournful howl of my wolf inside my head.

I vowed not to touch her.

Why can I not resist the temptation of her flesh, even with the guilt of man's religion bearing down on me. It worked four-hundred years ago when she was Sophia Alekseyevna, my sweet and fierce Sophia, and I swore not to mark and claim her in this life. I knew then everything had to change.

We couldn't keep living these lives over and over, with no progress to breaking the curse on her. The curse I created. I did my penance, and it paid off, even though I didn't get to see it. I heard all about Ekataryn, the greatest ruler of both the Russia and the Wolves. August, Vasily, and

Grigori had almost gotten her to the peak of ascension in that lifetime.

She was once again the Queen of Wolves, though called the Tsarina as befitted the time. She lived a long and mostly peaceful life for once in a thousand years. All because I wasn't there. When August told me the stories of his time at her side I was both relieved and disappointed I couldn't see her come into her power.

But she hadn't truly regained her magic.

Not like she had just now.

I was in awe of her. In five thousand years, a hundreds of lives lived and relived, I hadn't seen such magic and power manifest in her. She was truly Goddess touched. I had forgotten.

I watch as she heals Grigori's wounds, brings him back from death, as if she's doing nothing more than plucking a summer flower for herself. As if marking her, tasting her for the first time in hundreds of years wasn't enough, my body responds even more to this display of her true self.

My cock is so hard that it's painful. My wolf pushes me to finish my bond with her, to claim her as she wants me to, our bodies joined. The wolf's knot pulses at the base of my member, begging to be touched, stroked, buried in her sweet body.

I've already broken my vow not to touch her. I could not refuse her need to be marked. But I must deny us both that final connection between her and I.

She's not ready. Nor am I.

I know it's a lie the moment I think it.

Best not to even let those old wounds into my mind now that we are linked. I push all thoughts of the past away and concentrate on the here and now. With one final mental chastisement of myself for the way my hands shake with wanting to touch her beautifully naked and plush body, I pick up the discarded robes on the dirt floor and bring them over.

Grigori is alive. He breaths, his heart beats, but he is unconscious and in this state, even his wolf can't push through to shift and finish healing him. He's been touched by Hell and I can only pray that August and Vas are better off.

I lay the robes over her shoulders and then get down on the floor with her. She's trying to lift Grigori so she can lay his head on her breast, and it's interesting to me how she can use her strength to stave off death, but doesn't realize she can do anything else with her gifts.

"Let me help you, my lady." I'm careful with my words, and I feel stiff and clunky next to her charm.

She smiles and I'm dumbstruck by grace. She's had to beg me to help her save a life and I am ashamed. Of so much.

Together we lift Grigori, and she pushes one hand into his hair to hold his head to her, and puts her other arm around his shoulder. I want nothing more than to surround them both and hold them as if I'm pressing two broken pieces of my heart together. She is my queen, he is my alpha.

He may deny it, but if not for him, none of us would be

in her service. He chose us so that she could share her gifts from the Goddess. I give in one more time and fold them both into my arms.

"Thank you, Father." The words are quiet and solemn and for once I don't have a reply.

For just this moment, I will revel in her light and pretend I haven't destroyed her.

We sit together for a long time, and yet her light does not fade. She is glowing from within now, just as if she is the moon herself and only the passing of the month could dim her light. But there is no time passing in this prison, and I could be content to stay and hold her for an eternity.

In this peace I could hide from the reality of what is waiting for me when she learns the truth. No amount of prayer or even self-flagellation will save me from her punishment when she comes into her full powers. In trying to save her and keep her safe, I have failed not only her, but all of our people.

I can't forgive myself, why would she?

She knows that I'm stewing deep in thought. I can feel her mind pressing against mine. She's gentle, like the caress of moonlight on night blooming flowers. I keep my mind closed to her, but she is like an open book, wanting to know if I'm okay.

I never will be, but she doesn't need that burden. Instead I distract her with questions I don't want the answers to. "What did you remember, *boginya*?"

She's quiet for a long minute, thinking, letting memories flash through her mind. "Us."

I nod, pressing her to say more. "I understand now why you're drawn to religion. You're longing for the oldest of days."

I can hardly breathe. Does she remember all the way back to our first life together, when I found my calling in serving her?

"But what I don't understand is that so long ago, you were mine. You shared my bed and my heart. You want to recapture that as much as I do. Religion shouldn't be the thing that keeps us apart, but that which brings us together." Her voice is like the sweet whispers of a lover in the dark, but her words stab me. Her fingers caress the prayer beads wrapped around my wrist in a reverence no one else could understand.

It's time I got up and put some space between us, but I can't. I haven't held her in so long, and now that I have her body pressed to mine, I can't let go. "Any attempt to explain won't make sense. Just know that what I do is always in your best interest."

Her silence is recriminating enough for my non-answer. She strokes Grigori's hair and I feel her mind and magic at work again. "That's a load of crap, Father."

Well, fuck.

The power she's regained is not only in her magical abilities, but in her soul too. I have spent many a long night roaming the woods of our prison island simply to avoid thinking about how much I love her. She fights so hard in each reincarnation, against all odds. When she finally finds that inner strength, that's when I lost my heart to her each and every time.

Except once.

I glance over and see the mark I've made on her skin still swirling with the mating magic. Just as the other three have, this bite will form into an intricate design like a tattoo on her skin, that represents me and my role in her life. Even thinking about marking her reawakens the wolf inside and my instinctual need to claim her. No matter how much I will my body to still, my cock grows again and my pulse quickens.

All because of her sass and the way she's no longer afraid to call me out.

"It is. But we have bigger worries at the moment. Once Grigori is awake, we must find out if he was able to pull August and Vasily from Hell. I worry for all of our souls if he hasn't."

She allows me change of subject, but I know we aren't done. Someday soon I will have to own up to all my...crap.

Taryn presses her lips to Grigori's brow. "I don't think he's getting any better. I don't know what else to do for him. I wish you would just teach me about my magic and how to use it. I miss them, and I want them back. I need for us all to be together." Her voice is gentle, but her frustration buzzes in my mind.

"As Vasily explained, we have tried that before, and with catastrophic consequences. You must discover the gifts of the Goddess yourself, just as you did today."

Her mind goes to work again and I both dread and

revel in her train of thought. "When I figured out that you should mark me."

"Yes."

"But you won't claim me as August and Vasily did." It's not a question.

"No." Not yet. I withdraw but she grabs my arm and holds me to where I can't move without outright rejecting her touch.

"But you'll do... other stuff with me. Like you did when I mated August and Vasily."

I want to say no, but I can't. I indulged in the sins of the flesh during both of her matings. She couldn't know, but I'd done the same off on my own in the woods when I should have been praying for absolution. I dream of touching my cock to her lips, of seeing her come with such ecstasy that I can hardly breath.

I can't say any of that so I say nothing at all. But she sees me. Down to my very soul.

Taryn nods and strokes Grigori's hair some more and I'm fucking jealous of his broken unconscious state. She nods in understanding of everything I am.

"You all say I have to figure this out on my own. Well, here's what I've deduced. The Dark Prince isn't getting any better now that my fancy fit of magic is over. I also understand that there is power in the connection and bond I have with each of you. Am I wrong?"

My chest constricts but I push out the answer. "You're not."

"There is power and magic in sex, isn't there? Not just

fucking, but sharing our bodies because it's an expression of our deep, abiding love."

A whisper in both of our minds answers before I can. *Yes.*

No. If I could quiet Grigori's mind, I would. I don't want him giving her any ideas. But it's too late. Her clever mind is already sending me images of what she wants and what she thinks will happen.

"I need him to get better, Father. We both do. I know I said I wouldn't ask for more, but if it can help me access more magic and heal him so that we can save August and Vasily from Hell, we have to, don't we? There are lots of ways to have sex that doesn't involve--"

"I know, *boginya.* I know exactly how you like to be touched, and what will make you whimper with need. I can deny myself, but I can deny you very little." I have tried.

"I... I don't want you to think that this is enough. Someday when you're ready, I want you to fulfill the claim and make me your mate under the moon and stars. If you can't do that, then I will try to find another way to learn more magic."

I take her hand and kiss her palm. "All I am is yours. It is my failing, not yours that keeps us apart. I swear to you when the day comes when you no longer allow me this vow of chastity, I will be yours. It's always been in your power to break me and put me back together again."

I hear the echo in her mind of my words. *I don't want to break you.*

But she must and how well I know it. Until she does, I

will be whatever she needs me to be. Man, wolf, protector, almost lover. Because she knows her own power and it's almost time for her to ascend and reign again.

I move behind her and shift the robes so they cover Grigori's body, exposing hers to me. The ripeness of her hips, the dimples of her behind, and the soft rolls of flesh on her arms, back, and belly are so sensual that I reconsider for a moment what it would mean if I did claim her right here, right now. My wolf pushes to the surface, my fangs drop once again, and my cock pulses as if I'm already inside of her.

The wolf part of me wants to bury the knot deep inside of her, locking us together, until I'm sure she's mine once again. "Lay back against me, with his head cradled, and spread your legs for me."

She repositions herself, being careful not to jostle Grigori too much, until she is tucked against me with her ass against my cock and her knees spread. I'm reminded of the times when the two of us shared her body to bring her pleasure, his mouth on her pussy and my cock in her cunt, until she cried out with pleasure and her magic filled us all to repletion.

I'll never know days such as those again, so I will savor what I can have with her here and now. I will memorize every soft curve, every plump handful of belly, breast, and pussy. It's been so many hundreds of years since I've touched her, but my hands remember every little touch that turns her on.

I skim my knuckles across my mark on her throat and

my heart tremors to match the shivers of her skin. She leans into me and my cock presses against the seam of her ass. I cannot indulge in the lusciousness of that feeling or I won't be able to focus on what she needs.

Light as the petals of a flower, I trace the curve of her breast, and then tease her nipple until I grows hard as if reaching for my touch. The prayer beads rattle as they too caress her skin. She lets out the softest sigh and the blue sparkle of the magic of the moon dances across her skin, trailing my every touch.

I want to take my time with her, but I feel the push of Grigori's mind, wanting me to hurry. He knows what it means that I'm willing to do this for him. It's not only for him.

I can feel the urgency of the news he brings from Hell, but he isn't actually strong enough to just tell me or Taryn. He needs me. It's been a long time since I felt that. I kid myself that he wants me around for my counsel, but we both know that it is I who wants to be near him and who needs his advice.

"You are so very beautiful, *boginya*. I am a lucky man who gets to see, touch, and bring you pleasure." I get the feeling from the way the soft pink of a blush crosses her cheeks and chest that she hasn't been told that often enough in her most recent life.

I will tell her as often as I can until she tosses me aside.

TARYN

I'm reveling in Father Joachim's touch. I feel guilty and dirty, and I've only felt this wanted two other times in my life, when August and Vasily took me as their mate and claimed me in our special chapel of trees in the forest. While Joachim isn't properly claiming me and we aren't in that same place, we are in a church of sorts, and that feels right.

I didn't know until I used my magic to heal the prince where we are. This dungeon in the ground could be anywhere. But as the power inside of me swells with each of Joachim's caresses, our minds connected and, I see so much more than I imagine either of them want me to.

I lean into Father Joachim's touch, to where he is teasing my breast. I love it and want so much more from him at the same time. "Please, Father."

Even those two simple words feel dirty when I say them

like that, and he responds with a push of pure need into my mind.

I don't wait for him to hesitate and I grab his wrist, clasping his precious prayer beads, and drag them it across my belly and down between my legs. I'd have some guilt for pushing him, but I can full well feel the hard length of his cock pressing against my butt. Vasily had taken me there and it fulfilled every forbidden desire I had, until now.

I want Father Joachim to claim me in that same way. In fact, I want each one of my wolves to give me their bodies in every way possible. I want them alone, I want them in pairs, I want all four touching, tasting, teasing, and making me come, at the same time.

To make that happen, I have to save them all first. I would heal the prince, I would rescue August and Vasily, and I would draw Father Joachim out of his self imposed prison of punishment, and I would love them all until there was nothing left of their hurts and heart aches.

Another shot of power sizzles low in my belly and the marks on my neck burn, not with pain, but with passion. "Touch me, Joachim. I need you."

I need you to love me. I don't say those words, but there are no secrets between us in this moment. Not secrets of mine anyway.

"You're so wet. I wish I was inside of you right now." The words rasp out like an ardent prayer.

Is he saying that just to amp up the lust and thus the

magic or does he really want to break his vow right here, right now? "Then do it. Take me and make me your mate."

He groans and drops his mouth first to my head, giving me a kiss to the crown of my hair, then my temple, drags his lips and teeth down my neck and scrapes right over my mark. He bites into that same place again and as he sinks two of his fingers inside of me, the beads light up, glowing as if in approval of what we're doing.

"Oh, oh God - sorry Father." The words escape. Any filter I had left is gone.

He crooks his fingers inside of me, pressing his knuckles against the sweetest spot that I shake with the thrill of it. "Never apologize for taking your pleasure from me."

He rocks his palm against my pussy, the beads tickling the patch of hair on my mons, until I spread my legs even wider and his hand slides over my clit. The light in the room bounces around as if I am shooting off fireworks or lightening. The prince moans against my chest and his eyelashes flutter over my skin.

The magic is working, just as I knew it must. He is waking up. "More, Father, more."

I ask for what I want, what the prince needs, and what Joachim needs to give. His cock thrusts against me and his fingers mirror the movement. With each jerk of his hips, he sends me higher and higher. I can almost imagine his cock and not his fingers are buried inside of me.

"Let go, b*oginya*. Give everything you have to Grigori.

He needs you." His own words of the same sentiment echo in his mind. *I need you.*

But the prince doesn't need me to give him more. He awakens with a howl, his eyes alight with the sparkling blue magic of the moon. Before I can even breathe out gratitude that he is healed and returned to us, he twists in my arms and takes my nipple into his mouth. He suckles as if he is drinking in the magic from this joining and it pushes me higher, closer to climax than I've ever been, without going over the edge. I feel as though I could touch the moon and stars, floating among the heavens, the Gods and Goddess jealous of my rapture.

I throw my head back, reveling in the feeling of having two of my mates here with me, sharing my body, pushing us all into such perfect bliss.

The Dark Prince grabs me by the waist and crawls between my legs. "Do you like having his fingers in your cunt, pretty princess? Are those damned prayer beads rolling across your hard clit?"

His words are a low growl and he stares down to where Father Joachim is pleasuring me. "It's been far too long since he gave into these sins of the flesh."

"Yes, and yes." I pant the words both as an answer and a cry because I am so close to coming I can do nothing more. The way he looks at what Father Joachim is doing to me, makes me want even more of this delicious drug called sex magic.

The prince licks his lips and then looks up at Father Joachim. Some quiet but meaningful communication passes between them and I want to know what, but not enough to ask anyone to stop touching me. This is just supposed to be a way to help me access the magic inside of me, but just because I'd healed the prince, doesn't mean I want Father Joachim to stop.

It doesn't take but a moment for me to learn what they have in store for me. The prince presses two of his fingers into his mouth, wetting them, then he puts his hand between my legs too and pushes inside of me alongside Father Joachim. "Have you truly found the power inside of you? Do you remember who and what you are?"

How am I supposed to remember or think of anything when two of the hottest men on the planet are double-teaming to make me come? When one's fingers withdraw, the other pushes in and my body is going crazy for it.

They aren't even taking their own pleasure. Both their cocks are hard and pressing against me, but neither are doing anything to make themselves come.

There is definitely access to this sex magic in what they were doing to me, but I can feel the potential for so much more. If we could just join our bodies as one, then I know, I know with all of my heart and soul, I would remember everything.

I reach up and wrap one arm around the prince's neck, drawing him down and into a kiss. He bites my lip on one side and then the other. "No, no, princess. You don't get anything more from me unless you can tell me you're ready to break your damned curse and take back the power stolen from you."

Father Joachim wraps his other arms around my waist and holds me tight against his body. I think he too is lost in the magic. Neither of them stop thrusting their fingers inside of me, and yet, the tension won't break, I can't yet come.

"I. Am. Powerful." It's so hard to get the words out because I can hardly breathe. "I. Am...."

"What Taryn, what are you?" The wolf in him is so close to the surface I can see it in his eyes.

I want so badly to give him the answer he wants, but I don't know. I've found the place where the magic in me lives. With a little practice, I even think I can wield it without going out of control and hurting anyone. But while I have more memories than an hour ago, there are still so many holes in my Swiss cheese of a brain and I can sense the Nothing, the shadow blocking out the most important part of me.

So I say the only thing I know to be true. "I am yours."

Darkness flashes across his face, as if a cloud has passed over the moon. He withdraws his fingers and sits back on his heels, pulling his body so far away from me, I can feel the cold between us. "You're not mine until you know who and what you are. You're so fucking close I can taste it on you."

I want to cry out that I could know everything if only they would take this sex magic to the next, much more important level. I don't get that chance.

The Dark Prince stands, and throws the robes across

my body. He sneers and then growls at Father Joachim. "Finish her."

There's an edge to his voice I've never heard before, and Father Joachim reacts to it too. His hips jerk against me, thrusting his cock between my legs, but only to slide between my thighs and not inside of me. He lowers his lips to my ear and whispers. "Come for me, *moy malenkiy agnets.*"

My little lamb.

The moment he calls me that, I know he is firmly back in the arms of his God. Even though he's thrusting his cock between my slick thighs, everything has changed. To late for me to pull away, I give in to what my body has been waiting for and let the orgasm pour over me. Wave after wave of terrible pleasure courses through me and the only joy I take is the splash of Father Joachim's seed on my thighs and his tight grunt as he too comes.

I close my eyes and lean into him and say a prayer of my own, letting the words wash over both of them. *You are mine, I am yours.*

When the final tremors of my orgasm subsides, I listen to the harsh rapid breaths behind me. My senses are wide open now, as if I am in my wolf form, even though I am not. Everything in the room is clearer to me. I can see each individual speck of dirt, feel the tiniest of rocks digging into my knees. The smell, not only the death and evil that invaded this space, but the foul mood of the Dark Prince, and the guilt of Father Joachim are potent in the air. As is the new chill that wasn't there before.

I can taste the magic we performed by joining and exalting in joining our bodies and minds together, and that's what I grasp onto. I let that satisfaction swirl around and around, and when I open my eyes, the prince is staring down at me with a scowl, but also surprise.

Ha. So there, princey poo. I have learned something about myself. I wasn't lying when I said I am powerful. He's the one who got me to believe it.

Father Joachim kisses my temple and pulls the robes up and over me. I love how he's doing is best to take care of me, even under the scrutiny of the prince. While I know he has retreated back to the place in his mind where he isn't allowed to have feelings for me, we made strides toward each other. I'll take the win.

I turn into his embrace and give him the lightest of kisses to his throat. He hisses, but tries to hide it. I know what I'm doing in choosing this particular spot. That's the place he'll carry my mark someday. I'm simply saving it for later.

Then I lift his arm and kiss the beads wrapped around his wrist. I can taste myself on them, and his eyes go wide at my blatant attention to his sacred symbol of prayer and worship. The way he rolled those beads across my clit when he was thrusting his fingers inside of me is a much better use, in my opinion. "Your God may have hold on your conscience, but your heart and soul is mine. Our love will be your religion, when you are ready."

He turns his face away, and I let him. This has been a lot for him today. While he recovers, I will move my attention to my Dark Prince of Wolves. He's pretending to examine the damage I wrought on one half of his carefully constructed prison. But the conflict in his heart is as clear as if I am reading a book.

I pad across the dirt to him and slug him in the arm.

He doesn't even flinch and I know I haven't hurt him. That wasn't the point anyway.

He picks up a melted piece of metal that used to be the latch of the cell door. "What, pray tell, dear princess, was that for?"

"I think you know. Don't do that to me again." I wish he would look at me, but if he wants to push my buttons some more, then fine. I can play his game. I have his number now, he just doesn't know it.

He tosses the lock to the ground like so many other pieces of detritus. "I won't have to if you'll break the curse."

I'm down for some you're-an-asshole- banter. "I would if you and the good Father would do what I want."

He half laughs half scoffs. "It doesn't work that way."

You know what, I'm done with this I'm a man-wolf, I know better than you, little princess bullshit. The prince has intimidated the hell out of me since the first day. But I just saved his god-damned - sorry Father - life. If that doesn't put us on equal ground, nothing does. "It works however I want it to."

That gets his attention and he finally turns his head and looks at me. "Does it now?"

"Yes." We stare at each other for a good long minute and something new passes through his eyes. It's either relief or respect. I'll take either or. "Now tell me what happened to you and what news of August and Vasily."

Uh-oh. The eyebrow raise of disdain again. There goes my R-E-S-P-E-C-T. "None of that it matters."

I need to add some more creative swearing to my vocabulary to deal with the prince, because oh my God - sorry Father - isn't going to cut it. "Of course it matters, you boob. I need as much information as I can get if I'm going to rescue them from Hell."

"You?" He folds his arms and the other eyebrow goes up.

I fold mine, mirroring him. "Yes, you couldn't, so I will."

That ought to get his goat, or wolf as the case may be. I think I see him smile, but I won't tell him that.

He waves me toward the steps in an invitation to leave. "Then let me know when we leave for Hell. But I suggest you practice using your magic without someone else's hands between your legs. You're going to need every advantage you can get if you're going to take on the God of Chaos and risk angering the Goddess of Hell.

GRIGORI

*S*he thinks she's going to take on Hell all by herself. Ha. She's either got more hubris than I do, which will get her ass burned to a crisp, or she's finally found her fierce fighting spirit.

Warrior, fighter, protector. Those are supposed to my job. Mine and the rest of the Guard. She's the one we fight for. But if she's this close to remembering who she truly is, the Queen of the Wolves, Goddess touched, wolf cursed, then she's going to need everything she can to prepare for the battle ahead.

Especially if we're going back to Hell. I don't like that Nergal has a hard on for my princess. What has him interested in the affairs of wolves? Is this just a five thousand year old vendetta for the goddesses gift when our people pushed him and his demons back into Hell? It feels like somethings more, something new.

"Can we please get out of your red room of pain and get

working on our plan to rescue August and Vasily?" Taryn motions to the stairs.

"Red? If anything you've turned my dungeon blue." Her light is everywhere now. I have to guard myself from basking in her radiant glow. I can't imagine even standing next to the Goddess herself could feel anymore resplendent.

"I read it in a book in some lifetime. I used to like to read, you know."

Oh, I know. I spent hours reading poetry and philosophy to her when she was Katherine the Great. The first and last time I saw her even close to reclaiming her throne. Until now.

"I don't have any books and you don't have time to read." I've already made too many mistakes from our past with her. Poetry isn't going to win us the upcoming battle.

She rolls her eyes at me and looks to Joachim for solidarity. He's withdrawn into himself completely. I'm surprised he hasn't shifted into his wolf form to avoid talking to either of us all together. Although, he's marked her now and she's in his head.

He moves to the stairs without looking at either of us, and I get the feeling he'd bolt if he could.

"Come, we have work to do." I push the trapdoor open, busting the lock that should prevent anyone from getting out from this side.

"I already came, I think it's your turn." Taryn sashays her way up the stairs as if she owns the place.

If I'd known all it took was some orgasms to bring out

the sass in her, maybe I wouldn't have needed my dungeon. No, no. I will not fuck her, I will not put my face between her legs, or better yet, make her sit on my face while I fuck her with my tongue until she's shaking and weak. I will not fuck that sweet and sassy mouth of hers, and I will not claim her under the light of the full moon.

Not until I know he is safe.

She needs to grow in her powers if we're going to take on Hell.

I don't want her anywhere near Nergal and his forces of Hell, but I have a feeling there won't be any choice. I've seen this determination in her before. She'll burn down the world to reclaim her rightful place and protect her people.

This world needs to burn, especially this prison island. I just thought we would be fighting the Volkovs to win our freedom, not the forces of hell. Perhaps they are one in the same. The portals they use to transport their prisoners here and to keep us contained are of the shadow. That means someone made a deal with a demon because no mortal wolf can control that element without help from a God or Goddess.

I'd like to blame that dickface, Rasputin, but even he isn't as old as this prison the Volkovs have been using for centuries. No someone either long ago or much older made this Hell on Earth. If Taryn is to ascend, I need to find out who and why to make sure her life and power is never taken from her again.

Joachim and I follow her up the stairs of my destroyed little dungeon. In the cloudy spring light, I see Joachim flinch at being back in the shell of the church. For a brief moment when I first awakened, I thought finally he was ready to discard the mantle of protection he wears in the form of religion. I was sure she'd won him over. But he has retreated to that place again.

I root out some worn and tattered robes so that he can cover himself. His body got the gratification I've denied myself, yet both of us are still hard. I don't think my cock will ever rest until I've buried myself in Taryn's body and claimed her for my own.

My body and soul ache for her, my wolf is chomping and snarling at me for denying that pleasure. I will not do it until she is ready. Only when she is strong enough to save herself, will I bow at her feet, and ask her to be mine. That has to be the difference this time.

I can't protect her, as much as I'm driven to.

"Okay, who wants to practice some magic so we can go to Hell and rescue my lovers." Taryn claps her hands and rubs them together. "That is not a sentence I ever thought would come out of my mouth."

She flicks her fingers and shots of sparkling magic surge through the rubble of my lair. Moon flowers spring up turning the fearsome ruins into a nature reclaimed sanctuary. How, after everything that has happened to her, is she filled with such light?

Joachim takes the robes, slips them on and moves his prayer beads from his wrist back to his waist. He busies himself with his task and doesn't look at me, but his voice rings clear in my mind. *Because she knows her darkness is safe with you, Guard of the House of the New Moon, Dark Prince of Wolves.*

A new bond has forged between the two of us. Something we haven't shared since our last shared life with her. Since the last time we shared her body. I don't want him in my head, unguarded, listening to my thoughts. *I cannot protect her from the darkness any longer, priest.*

I want to poke and push him away. His failings only remind me of my own.

It is not the darkness of others, the world, or even Hell she needs protecting from, but her own. The rest of us get to see her light and bathe in her love. You are the only one strong enough to bear the shadow in her soul.

My hands and fingers go dumb. The rustling of the wind in the trees goes quiet against the ringing in my ears. My wolf surges up as if I'm in danger and the shift pushes at my skin.

In a thousand lifetimes, no one has ever said as much to me. I was chosen to protect her at her weakest, when there is no light from the moon, because I was the strongest warrior. I became her Dark Prince. But what if all this time, it wasn't my job to keep her safe from the darkness, but to help her embrace it?

Isn't that what I've been pushing her to do, locking her in my dungeon in the dark, and forcing her to face her demons all on her own.

I look over at her, glowing for us all to see. Even in the burned rubble of this once beautiful but tainted church, others will be drawn to her light. How can they help it?

Am I the reason her powers have been hobbled in life after life? My chest is caving in, my heart stutters and has forgotten how to beat the blood through my veins. This is why I've been so angry for so long.

No. That fault lies with... that doesn't matter.

There's more he needs to say, because it does matter. I will tackle that later. Much, much later. Once I remember how to breathe, live, and do my duty to her once again. *Why have you never said anything before?*

We both know there are some lessons that must be learned, not taught. I only speak now because you've realized already what you have to do. You've been doing it since she arrived in our keep once again. I'm the one who didn't understand that until today.

It took me taking her life and being thrown into supernatural prison to break my own soul open to see my mistakes. All this time on the island, I thought I was rebelling against our fate as her Wolf Guard, but my true nature was just trying to get through, just as hers has been.

I don't know how to... her strength is in her light, her magic comes from the Goddess gift of the moonlight.

Without darkness, there is no light. She needs you just as much as the three of us combined. That's why you're our alpha.

An honor I tried to give up.

She's never embraced the dark side of her nature. I've always protected her from that.

Not always. Do you remember when she was Olga of Kyiv?

A life from long ago that lives among the other regrets

in my heart. I died, killed by her enemies, leaving her vulnerable.

She burned down half of old Russia to avenge your death. Her vengeance was glorious, but frightening. Left unchecked, her darkness flowed like rivers of blood.

I shouldn't be able to, because she's always been such pure light to me, but I absolutely can imagine her wreaking a horrible wrath on the Derevlyanins. I found I liked the idea.

I didn't know.

I didn't know. She avenged my death, she brought me back to life, and I couldn't even deign to do my own duty for her.

You do now. Do better than I have. Go, claim her, and help her ascend to her rightful place.

She cannot ascend until all four of us have taken our places by her side. I am chastising myself as much as I am Joachim. If I would have done as he asked when she first arrived, shown up for her mating ceremony with August, and joined them, we could have... no, we all have lessons to learn in this life with her.

I pray, which we all know I don't do, but I'll make the exception now. I pray that Joachim is close to learning his as well. As his alpha I should have been helping him just as much as her. I vow to be better.

She makes me a better man, wolf and guardian. As is her right. I've forgotten that. But I won't again.

I move quietly to the part of the sanctuary she's in considering how to tell her that I understand my duty now without revealing too much. A line of her moonflowers pop up along the path ahead of me.

I want to bow at her feet, kiss the very ground she walks on and genuflect before her. That is not what she needs from me. If I am to help her embrace her darkness, assist her in using that to defeat the forces of Hell to rescue our brethren, then guide her back into her light, she doesn't need submission from me.

I too must embrace the shadow in my soul. That's what has brought me this far, and I can't be afraid of hurting her now.

Because she is strong, she can save herself. I'm only here to be by her side as she does.

She's using the soft side of her magic and not only are the flowers blooming, but the trees are growing back out of the scorched ground filling in where the wooden and brick walls used to be. It was never church buildings that she loved, just places of worship.

Left over, I'm sure, from when we worshipped her.

I drag her against the nearest tree she's pulled into being, and clasp her tight in my arms. Her eyes sparkle with surprise and lust. For me.

I've made love to her, fucked her, claimed her as my mate in more lives than I can count. I've always wanted it to perfect for her. I've always been gentle, putting her pleasure first. I understand now, that was wrong. She needs me as harsh and punishing as her lover, as in her guard.

Taryn wraps one leg around the back of mine and

smiles up at me with her saucy, knowing grin. "What's this, my Dark Prince? Couldn't get enough of me?"

Her. Dark. Prince.

I growl and shove my hips against hers, ripping the robes she's wearing open to her round goddess's body is exposed to me. "Never."

Her eyes goes dark and she licks her lips. The scent of her arousal overwhelms me and my wolf pushes to the surface, wanting to claim her in response. Hot damn. My sweet princess wants me to be rough with her. What the fuck have I been doing for the last five-thousand years?

The shoddy mark I placed on her neck sings out to me to bite her again. I wrap my hand around her throat, caressing the symbol of my wolf in the darkened moon with my thumb. She lets out a sensual sigh and her eyes flutter shut.

"Mark me, claim me, make me yours."

I'm not sure if Taryn is saying these words to me, or my ancient queen.

Dusk is upon us and the ever present clouds in sky part. Rays from the moon shine down on us both and she glows as only a true mate does. This is not her goddess given gift of moonlight on her skin, it's the manifestation of our fate sparkling, tempting me to her, something no one could resist.

"You are mine, my queen. I won't fail you again." I lower my mouth to her skin and scrape my teeth across the ragged mark.

Her fingers lace into my hair, just as they did when she

was healing me, but this time she isn't gentle either. She grips my scalp, scraping her nails from the crown down, holding me to her. "More, my prince, more."

Saliva drips from my fangs, my mouth literally watering for the taste of her. I shoot my hand up from where I've had it around her throat to her hair and wrap her locks around my fist. I tug hard, forcing her to expose her most vulnerable soft flesh to me. I could rip out her artery with one bite, and yet she trusts me.

Before I bite down, I slide my hand around her thick thigh and hoist her up so she has to wrap her legs around my waist. My cock slides through her already wet folds, my tip caressing her clit. My wolf is begging to bury every hard inch of my dick so deep into her cunt that already the knot at my base is pulsing. I thrust against her, not into her to tease us both. "I'm going to mark you, claim you, and then I'm going to fuck you so hard you black out from screaming my name."

She sucks in a hissed breath, then does the opposite of what I told her she would. She whispers my name. For the first time since I took the innocent life she lived as Anastasia Romanov, she says my name. "Grigori."

I am lost. I bite down, sinking my fangs into her skin, tasting her blood, and arousal, and magic. She shatters in my arms, her body going tight with the first orgasm. It's not enough for either of us.

She says my name again, whimpering her need for me. "Grigori."

I lick the wound reopened and push the healing power

of my wolf to close the bite. My cock throbs and grows harder watching the tattoo symbol swirl and connect with the others on her skin. I wish the rest of her guard was here with us now to witness this claim. *Joachim, come, perform the ancient ceremony and witness my claiming.*

He is beside us before I even finish the thought, but I don't wait for the ritualistic words. I grip her thigh tight, knowing there will be a bruise there tomorrow, and slide my hand around her throat once again. She bites her lip and stares deep into my eyes, her magic swirling between us, and I thrust my cock all the way to the hilt in one rough push of my hips.

The beautiful blue glow of her light, goes from bright like lightening to dark like the shadow on fire. I withdraw and shove in again, harder, until I'm filling her body, working my knot into her tight cunt. I fuck her hard and she moans with each ever-deeper thrust.

Never once does her gaze leave mine. Her pupils are blown, and taking over the whites of her eyes. Her cunt pulses around me and her body shakes, on the verge of another climax. Then she lifts her arm, palm to the sky, and the world goes dark as the moon shining down eclipses and we are baptized in her utter darkness.

TARYN

Grigori, my Dark Prince has finally come to me. He's marked me, and is claiming me. I'm sure in all of my lives, I've never experienced sex like this. He's fierce, rough, and it's exactly what I need. What I didn't even know I needed.

His dark desires wash over me, through me and bring up the shadows buried deep in my soul. They balance out my light and I am finally able to push away the Nothing left in my mind. Magic and shadow, light and dark swirl around us.

I remember.

I remember everything.

I remember too much.

All my lives, all the loss, all the love, good and bad, heaven and hell are whooshing through my mind and it's threatening to drown me. I don't even know what I'm doing when I raise my hand to the sky. I just know I need to release the rising tide of magic bubbling up from centuries and centuries of lessons learned.

More power than any mortal being can possess flows through me, and I am filled with hope and rage. If I can't control the flow of magic, I don't know what's going to happen, but it won't be good. I need something to ground me and it can't be just anything.

I need my Wolf Guard.

Grigori, my Dark Prince of Wolves is with me, inside of me, connecting his soul with my own. He is my chosen one, the strongest of them all, the one who guides all the others. He is fearsome and yet broken. I've put too heavy a burden on him and he doesn't think he's strong enough.

I can hear his thoughts, and he truly believes in his heart, that he has failed me. They all do. Because they couldn't protect me from the evil in our world, the chaos around us, they think they are not worthy.

What they don't understand is it is I who is supposed to be protecting them.

Without thought, I reach out and touch Grigori's soul. The wolf inside of him howls and his body explodes into pure pleasure. His cock sinks deep into me and the wolf's knot locks into place as he spills his seed into my channel. We are one and while this is meant to be his claim on me, I am the one who asserts my dominion over his soul.

He is mine.

They all are. Every person on this island... oh save the Unicorn and the Lion, are mine. But two are special to me. I reach out to Joachim's soul and pull him to me. He's saying the words I taught him so long ago, to bind us all together.

"We gather together in this, our sacred circle to honor the Goddess of the Moon who bestowed upon us the very nature of our wolves and gave us the light by which to find out way to our true fated mates."

He is using the old ritualistic words, if not the old language. None of us have spoken them in thousands of years. "If your fated mate be here, declare your claim on them and let your pack know that they are yours and that you belong to them."

He takes Grigori's hand from around my throat and places it over my heart. My prince is still breathing hard and it takes him a minute to shake of the euphoria of our mating. But in a moment, he nods and says the words I need to hear from him. "Taryn, I Grigori, Dark Prince of Wolves, Guard to you of the House of the New Moon, claim you as my mate. You are mine and I am yours for all time."

His words and his claim, pull me down from the heights of overwhelm and help me focus on him and this moment. Father Joachim takes my hand and places it on Grigori's chest. The words flow from me easily. Grigori, my guardian of the new moon and my darkness, I claim you as my mate. I am yours and your are mine for all time."

His chest shudders under my palm as old heart wounds knit back together. He swallows and takes a long, deep breath as if he hasn't had one in a long time. His cock surges inside of me, and the wolf's knot gluing us together throbs. He leans forward and brushes a soft kiss across my lips.

"Don't forget who you are to me, Dark Prince." I nip at the corner of my mouth with my teeth and he smiles like I've never seen him do before. There's dark promises in that grin. He squeezes my hip and shoves his other hand into my hair, gripping it tight in his fist once again. His mouth crashes down on mine and we are a mess of lips, teeth, tongues, all rolled into one fierce kiss.

Through the haze of this sensuality, I hear Father Joachim speak again. "Friends, join us in the sacred circle to witness the claiming and renew your own bonds."

Both Grigori and I look up, for the first time breaking eye contact with each other, and we are surrounded by everyone from the *derevnya*, including the new packs that joined us, and Maggie and Will.

Will gives us a salute, and Maggie says, "The eclipse darkened the island so that only your light could be seen. We thought we ought follow that beacon, and here we are, witness to your mating."

She winks and steps back, into the arms of her mate, the King of Scotland, and protector of the Tuatha Dé Danann. Strange. I know who these two beings are, but not why they are here. They do not belong to me, yet they are integral to my life. Maybe I don't remember everything yet.

Grigori throws back his head and howls his pride, his happiness, and his desire for me into the far reaches of the night. Joachim joins his howl and the rest of the pack joins in, echoing through the night.

The howls resound through the sanctuary that makes up another new sacred circle of the moon, and each and every wolf lifts their voices up.

But two voices are missing.

I touch Grigori's face and he nods in understanding. His wolf is satisfied that we are once again connected soul deep and the knot recedes. He slips from me and lowers my feet to the ground. I slip out of the robe and hand it to him. I don't need it anymore.

With an easy swish of my fingers, I dress of moonflowers, knitted together with vines, covers me from head to toe. The magic I fought is now at my disposal and my powers are almost limitless.

Grigori dons the robes and then as one, he and Joachim kneel before me. Grigori says in a loud, clear voice, "All hail, Taryn, Queen of the Wolves."

A hush rolls across the gathered crowd and in a wave, everyone kneels and bows their heads to me. I allow them this moment of exaltation, but it's neither necessary or wanted. I may have lived a thousand lives, but not since that first life, when they were given the ability to shift, have I fulfilled my duty to them as Queen.

They've had to fight and scrabble for every scrap of dignity and respect, and not this proud lot of them have been imprisoned by false rulers. The days of the Volkovs are numbered.

"Stand and greet me as friend. I may have the gift of moon magic, but I am still the same woman you welcomed into your fold and helped to survive in this harsh prison."

The women I have come to think of as my girl gang are the first to break the spell and approach me. I open my arms to them and hope they aren't intimidated by who they think I am now. I may remember al my past lives, how to use my powers, and who I am, but that doesn't mean I don't need friends.

I look into each of their eyes, Alida, Killisi, Bridget, Jeanette, and even Maggie. I return to them the calm and confidence they lent to me when I first arrived in the *derevnya*. Maggie smiles and gives the other girls a shove forward until I'm wrapped up in a big group hug.

"We didn't know you were the Queen of Wolves, my lady. Sorry." Alida shrugs and blushes just a little.

"Well, to be fair. I didn't know either." That gets a good chuckle all around and I'm happy to be back in their fold. "I'll need more help, ladies. Are you up for bringing out the claws for me again?"

Bridget scoffs like I've asked something daft. "Of course. Anything for you."

"Good. Because you're going to need those fighting skills I've come to count on. My magic is powerful, but it has limits, especially when it comes to the evil forces of Hell. I can either fight, or I can protect everyone. I can't do both at the same time."

Killisi gave an eyebrow waggle and her wolf surged up, glowing in her eyes. "We can fight for you. It's fun kicking the asses of the baddies that have terrorized us for so long."

Grigori and Joachim joined us. I would be even more powerful with my fervent priest's claim on me too, but he's got a dark mark on his soul, that I will have to heal before he can accept my love again. That will be easier for me to tackle with the rest of my Wolf Guard at my side.

Grigori, with his mantle of alpha firmly back in place, put his hand on my lower back. "What are you planning, my Queen."

"Would everyone please stop calling me that? This is the twenty-first century, and not ancient Sumer. Just call me Taryn."

Maggie chuckled. "It's hard when they find out who and what you are, isn't it, love?"

"I mean, how do you all think I feel? A hot minute ago I was an amnesiac Hogwarts drop out?"

"Now, now, sweet queen, you don't look like a hog or have warts."

"Oh God - sorry Father - I forget how long you've been out of the real world. That is step two on my agenda. But first, we mount the rescue party to save August and Vasily from Hell. Raise your hand if you're tired of this cold Siberian winter and want a trip somewhere really, really hot."

Everyone around me put their arms in the air, but Grigori scowled at them all and they put them back down. "No one is going to Hell."

"I thought we were done with the whole you have to protect me from everything bit. That's my job now and we are getting August and Vasily back." I glowered at him and he sent me an image of me over his knee getting a spanking back into my mind.

Ooh. Fun. For later.

Joachim rolled his eyes at the two of us. Pretty sure he got that image thrust into his mind too. Sorry not sorry. He shakes his head and says, "If you truly have your powers back, you can open a portal to Hell and summon them back."

"Oh. Sweet." I know I just said I remembered everything, but that's a lot of memories to sort through in a short amount of time, so I'm giving myself some grace on not knowing all the things stored in the giant filing cabinets in the castle in my mind.

"Right. Let's do this." I raise my hands into the air, but before I let the magic flow, I pause just a moment. "Maybe you all should shift and get ready for battle anyway, because we've already had a run in with the dickhead of Chaos and some demons. They could also pop up while I'm getting August and Vasily."

In a flurry of popping bones and flying fur, a hundred wolves, ready to take on the forces of Hell, stand before me. It's good to be Queen.

"Ready, everyone?" I hold my hands up in the air again and call on the magic of the moon so bright in the sky.

My question is met by a chorus of howls. I'll take that as a yes. I give a little swirly, swirly, flick and swish and a shadow portal open before us all.

I feel August and Vasily's souls immediately and push my light through the portal to search them out and pull them back to me on this strange piece of the mortal realm.

There's some interesting magic in Hell that doesn't belong there.

I touch the minds wielding the elemental magic of the Goddess Inanna. I think I'll bring these two back with me too. Near the little fire witch, I find my wolves. My soul connects once again with theirs and fills in the holes left in my heart from their absence.

But my light has been noticed by the evil chaos. Damn. Before I can bring August and Vasily back, the great owl with his oily stained wings, and chaos in his heart burst up and out of the portal.

Grigori and Joachim jump in front of me. I must trust them to fight while I protect even though my instinct is to keep them safe. Ten wolves attack, and half are thrown free from Nergal's wings. He isn't fighting claw and beak like he did before. It's almost as if he's tethered by someone or something else.

A stream of demon wyrms pour out of the portal after him and right behind them are my lovers, my life, August and Vasily.

They attack the demons from behind while my army of wolves slaughter them from the front. It doesn't take long before the forest around us is covered in their oily stains of death. Gross. The only threat left is one large demon wyrm who has taken on the shape of a black dragon. He's being protected by August and Vasily. Grigori rushes over and stands with them.

My queen. This beast is different from the others. He wants only to escape Hell's grip on him and his brethren. Grigori shows me his interactions with this demon dragon while in Hell and August and Vasily back him up.

Fine. I have no beef with Dragons. "He can stay, but I have to close the portal. There's something darker coming."

I stare deep into the portal, and can see a dark spell tethering Nergal, the God of Chaos once used against me and my people to terrorize me into using my powers. But Nergal is just flying around, up above our heads, and isn't attacking anyone. Something tells me he's a few french fries short of a happy meal today.

Someone else is controlling him. The only being I can think of that has that kind of power is Ereshkigal, the Goddess of the Underworld, and his wife. I don't really want her popping out of hell to our little island. That would make this prison camp into a death camp. No, thank you.

I also see in the shadow, the face of a young woman. The fire witch. A dragon's daughter. I offer my light to her, but she shakes her head. She is not one of my people, so I can't force her to come along. She turns away from the portal and disappears.

Then it's time to shove Nergaly Wergaly back into Hell and close this sucker up before whatever is on the other side of his leash comes through.

I close my hands, willing the portal to close. It doesn't.

"Come on, come on. I'm all juiced up on love, so do as you're told shadow." I close my hands into fists, trying again to close the entry and exit to Hell.

No go.

And now I see why.

I'm not the only one holding it open.

A tall bearded figure, in black robes, with the stench of evil on him steps through the portal.

"Hello, Taryn. I wondered where my incompetent minions stashed you."

Rasputin?

He reaches his hand out of his robes and closes his fist the same as I did, but instead of closing the portal, his black magic grabs me by the neck and crushes my throat. Nergal swoops down and his claws did into my shoulders and he lifts me into the air and toward the shadow portal.

Oh, fuck no.

I'm not going down without a fight.

JOACHIM

I feel the very moment my Queen remembers the first life we all lived together. I was a lost and lonely soul back then, looking for any way to survive.

Grigori was my first savior, recruiting me to the priesthood of the Goddess of the Moon. I was in awe and wonder at the splendor of her temple. I learned to pray, I learned to fight to defend and protect her, and I learned to love.

I went from initiate to priest, without once ever seeing the Goddess herself.

I didn't need to, just the meaning she gave my life when I worshipped her, was enough. I could have lived a peaceful life and died happily bowing at the steps of her temple.

But then the demons attacked and Chaos reigned. Those I called friends and family were killed before my very eyes. We were terrorized because we loved our sweet Goddess.

Then she bestowed upon our people the ability to defend ourselves against the vile evil attacking us. Our bones broke and reshaped, our skin split and covered our fragile bodies with fur, and our nails became killing claws. We howled to the Moon in thanks and praise for her gift.

Forever more the people of the Moon didn't have to be afraid. But because she gave so much of herself to keep us all from harm, she floated down from the heavens, and become a mortal.

The Queen of the Wolves.

Grigori, as her Dark Prince, chose me, along with August and Vasily to be her Wolf Guard. We would live life along with her, and protect her from the harshness of the world.

She loved us, each and everyone, and we became her mates.

But as time passed, I grew scared. Our Queen was so vulnerable, even with the remnants of her magic to protect her. I decided to do something about it.

I have regretted everyday of my existence since then.

I have waited in fear for the day she would discover what I have done to curse her, and condemn me.

I deserve her punishment, even as I seek her love.

Today is the day she will know what I have done and forsake me.

She is powerful.

She is a Goddess once more.

NEED MORE of Taryn and her adventures with her Wolf Guard?

Get the finale book in the series - Undefeated

CAN'T WAIT? Grab this bonus chapter for this book when you sign up for my Curvy Connection newsletter.

ALSO BY AIDY AWARD

The Black Dragon Brotherhood

Tamed

Tangled

Twisted

Alpha Wolves Want Curves

Dirty Wolf

Naughty Wolf

Kinky Wolf

Hungry Wolf

Fate of the Wolf Guard

Unclaimed

Untamed

Undone

Undefeated

Curvy Temptation

Curvy Persuasion

The Curvy Seduction Saga

Rebound

Rebellion

Reignite

Rejoice

Revel

ACKNOWLEDGMENTS

Thanks to - JL Madore, Claudia Burgoa, Dylann Crush, and M. Guida. I appreciate all your help and patience as I burn hard. Special thanks to Becca Syme and her Better Faster Academy. Thanks for being my Tim Gunn.

I'm so grateful for my Amazeballs Writers who are always willing to get on and do writing sprints with me. I appreciate it more than you could know.

My Amazeballs Facebook group is so much of the reason I keep writing and I look forward to logging on every day and seeing what kind of fun and games we've got going on each day!

I am so very grateful to my Patreon Book Dragons!

I was was nervous starting a new kind of story and your comments kept me going when I doubted my own storytelling abilities.

Shout out to my Official VIP Fans!

Thank you so much for all your undying devotion for me and the characters I write. You keep me writing (almost) every day.

Extra Hugs to you ~

- Heather R.

- Jeanette M.
- Kerrie M.
- Frania G.
- Michele C.
- Killisi
- Janis W.
- Robin. O

And enormous thanks to my Official Biggest Fans Ever. You're the best book dragons a curvy girl author could ask for~

Hugs and Kisses and Signed Books for you from me!

- Helena E.
- Alida H.
- Daphine G.
- Danielle T.
- Bridget M.

ABOUT THE AUTHOR

Aidy Award is a curvy girl who kind of has a thing for stormtroopers. She's also the author of the popular Curvy Love series and the hot new Dragons Love Curves series. She writes curvy girl erotic romance, about real love, and dirty fun, with happy ever afters because every woman deserves great sex and even better romance, no matter her size, shape, or what the scale says.

Read the delicious tales of hot heroes and curvy heroines come to life under the covers and between the pages of Aidy's books. Then let her know because she really does want to hear from her readers.

Connect with Aidy on her website. www.AidyAward.com get her Curvy Connection, and join her Facebook Group - Aidy's Amazeballs.

Made in the USA
Columbia, SC
28 September 2023

23554821R10079